Last Chance Cowboy

Last Chance Ranch Book 2

Liz Isaacson

Chapter One

Adele Woodruff slid her hands down the front of the jeans she'd put on in the dressing room, wondering why she hadn't gotten a more physical job sooner. After all, working twelve hours a day on her best friend's ranch had proven to be the best weight loss solution she'd ever found.

She was down fifteen pounds now, and these jeans showed curves she'd forgotten she had. She turned and looked at her behind in the mirror, deciding these were definitely the jeans she needed. Adele was currently counting pennies to make sure she had the money necessary to pay her bills, but these jeans had practically been made for her body.

So she'd get two pairs. That was reasonable. She worked on a ranch now, for crying out loud, and while she'd only been there a few weeks, her clothes had taken a serious toll. The jeans she'd brought with her were ratty and perpetually dirty, so getting a couple of new pairs wasn't unreasonable.

If only her debt collectors understood what was reasonable and what wasn't. If only Hank, her no-good, used-to-be-stinking-rich ex hadn't put all of his expenses in her name and then skipped town. As one woman at a credit card company had told her several months ago, she didn't care who'd racked up the debt. The fact was, the account was in Adele's name, and the payment was due on the fifth of each month.

Each and every month.

She'd disputed a couple of the bigger cards and found some relief that way, but they'd only offered her a lower payoff amount, with a more aggressive payback schedule.

She pushed the thoughts of Hank and his monumental debt from her mind. She needed jeans and boots to work on the ranch, period.

Oooh, boots, she thought, and detoured over to the shoe department. So the two pairs of boots she bought weren't exactly what one might need to work with goats on a rescue ranch—or what Scarlett, the owner of Last Chance Ranch, hoped would become a rescue ranch. But Adele needed the ankle boots nonetheless.

With her purchases in the back of her car, she stuck the key in the ignition and sent up a prayer. "Come on," she whispered. "Please let it start quickly." She used to pray that she could get the sedan to start on the first try.

But she couldn't remember the last time that had happened, so her pleas to the Lord had changed into *just let it start before I melt in here.*

Sometimes that worked, and sometimes she had to get out of the car and take a break to breathe before trying again. Today, in the mall parking lot, God answered her prayers, because the car started on the third try.

"Thank you," she said, slapping the steering wheel. "This might actually be a new record." She flipped the car into gear and started toward the grocery store. She had dozens of ideas for her food videos, but she was on a very strict budget for them. Yes, her Instagram channel was fairly new, with only about a hundred and fifty videos. She posted a new one each morning, and that meant a lot of cooking in the evening. It meant shopping several times a week. It meant spending money she *almost* had.

But her popularity had been growing lately, especially as she focused more on feeding a ranch crowd than doing what some of the other foodie video channels did— anything and everything.

No, Adele wanted to be niched down, because the audiences there were hungry and loyal. The potential to stand out skyrocketed, and she hadn't seen anyone else doing Beef's Greatest Hits or Budget Meals for Two.

She'd done both of those, but now that she was on the ranch, she wanted to focus on a more country-style approach to cooking. Things that had to simmer and stew, like chicken pot pie or beef tips and gravy. She wanted to

3

do cowboy pizzas, and rustic desserts, and down-home cooking anyone could do.

Anyone with a single hotplate, the most expensive lights in Hollywood, and four video cameras, that was. She'd found all of the equipment from one of Hank's storage units several months back. After all, her name was on the lease, and she was the one they'd contacted when he'd stopped paying the bill. Her choice was to lose everything in the storage unit to an auction or come clean it out.

She'd gone and cleaned it out, finding several treasures—the lights and cameras had sparked her idea to start her own food videos, and she'd sold everything else to pay off one of Hank's cards.

Her channel made a little bit of money now, and she'd vowed to use only that income to buy the groceries she needed for the videos. She was putting a hundred percent of her earnings back into this business, but it was small and fledgling, and she believed in it.

She selected the cuts of meat she needed, then the vegetables, always planning and double-planning her menu to use a lot of the same items so nothing went to waste. She had a good stock of staples—flour, sugar, salt, garlic powder and other spices—by now, and most of her expenses went to the protein she was cooking, or the dairy aisle. Because wow, she'd never really paid attention to how expensive heavy cream was.

She knew now.

She checked out, her bill coming twenty dollars over

what she'd made the previous week. *It's okay*, she told herself. She'd make that twenty dollars back this week with her amazing apple turnover video and the watermelon gazpacho she had planned.

With the food in the backseat next to the boots and jeans, she got behind the wheel again, once again praying for a miracle.

She twisted the key. Nothing happened. Again and again, she tried and the engine just clicked. "Come on," she said, a hint of desperation in her voice. She wiped the back of her hand along her forehead and ignored the people walking by as they headed into the store.

Next time, she told herself as she tried again. And again. She started saying it out loud, but when she'd been trying to get her stupid car started for fifteen minutes, she left the key in the ignition and got out.

Frustration boiled within her. Why couldn't Hank have had a new Mercedes in the storage unit? She could've used that. Guilt immediately cascaded through her. She knew God had blessed her with the lights and filming equipment, and she'd spent hours on her knees thanking Him. So she couldn't be upset about what she didn't have.

And yet, she was.

She paced away from the car, the air hot in the parking lot. At least there was a breeze. The car had working air conditioning, if she could just get it started, but the windows didn't roll down. So she really couldn't sit in it for very long, trying to get the blasted engine going.

If she didn't get back up to the ranch soon, Scarlett would wonder where she'd gone. And Adele didn't want to explain anything, even to her best friend. No one knew about the foodie videos, and she wasn't ready to tell anyone yet.

She returned to the car, actually somewhat disappointed that no one had stolen it while she'd taken her walk around the parking lot. "They probably tried," she muttered. "And couldn't get it started."

She sighed as she got behind the wheel again. Yes, she'd lost some weight, but she had a lot more than fifteen pounds to lose to be considered anywhere close to thin. She left the door open and turned the key again. Counting in her head, she made it to ten, then twenty. She coached herself to get to thirty, then forty, then fifty before she gave up, got out, and kicked the tires.

She didn't make it to fifty, because the engine turned over on try number forty-six.

"Hallelujah," she said, reaching to pull the door shut. She really needed to get Scarlett's new cowboy-slash-mechanic to look at her car. But Hudson Flannigan had been so busy with projects around the ranch, and Adele didn't know him well enough to ask.

Besides, she couldn't pay him. That had kept her mouth shut too.

She flipped the car in reverse and slammed her foot on the gas pedal at the same time she checked behind her. Her car moved, and it seemed to be going at the speed of sound, especially when she saw the huge, white truck behind her.

A horn sounded. She slammed on her brakes. The sedan jerked to a stop. Or had she hit that truck?

Her heart beat in the back of her throat as she put the car in park and opened her door.

"What are you doing?" a man demanded, coming around the front of the truck to see if she'd hit him. She was wondering the same thing, but his condescending tone lit a fire inside her chest.

Or maybe that was this man's rugged good looks. His long legs and broad shoulders. That delicious cowboy hat he wore, revealing only the hint of sandy blond hair, neatly trimmed. His beard was cut close too, revealing a strong jaw Adele could grip while she kissed him.

She shook herself. Kissed him? What in the world was that? Adele was not interested in this pretty-boy cowboy, though her pulse testified that oh, yes she was.

The cowboy hat and boots were obviously for show, because his jeans looked like the ones she'd just purchased. Brand new. Not a speck of dust anywhere. The boots too, looked like he'd never stepped foot on a ranch, a boarding stable, or even dirt.

He wore a shirt in a lighter tint than summer grass, and he clearly had more money than he knew what to do with. When he looked at her, she forgot where she was and why she was so sweaty.

Sweaty. Oh, man, she was *so sweaty* from her fight with starting the car. Why couldn't she meet handsome men while she was dressed in a flirty skirt and with her makeup done just right?

Embarrassment crept through her, but she lifted her chin. This guy was no different than Hank. Sure, he had a black cowboy hat and a pair of boots Hank wouldn't be caught dead wearing, but other than that, he was exactly like her dirty, rotten ex-husband.

"I didn't hit your precious truck," she said.

"Came real close," he said.

"Yeah, well, real close and contact are two different things." She turned and started back toward her seat. He grabbed her arm, and dang, if that didn't send fireworks and a raging inferno of fury through her bloodstream.

She glared at his hand and then up into his eyes. "Get your hands off me. And move your truck. You're causing a traffic jam."

The cowboy removed his hand from her arm as if he'd been burned. He had the decency to look cowed by her. Embarrassed even, hopefully that he'd touched her without her permission.

"What's your name?" he asked.

"You don't need it," she said, getting behind the wheel and closing her door. At least the car was still running, the air conditioner blowing.

She looked in her rear-view mirror to see the big truck still blocking her and that delicious man still staring at her.

It was easier to glare than to smile, and besides, Adele was *not* interested in another billionaire boyfriend. Oh, no, she was not.

Chapter Two

C arson Chatworth didn't want to get in his truck and leave without getting that pretty woman's name. But she wasn't budging from behind the wheel of her car, and he really was causing a traffic flow problem in the parking lot.

He decided he didn't care. He'd been in California for approximately seventy-two hours and the traffic here was the worst he'd ever seen. Of course, anything was going to be worse than Gold Valley, Montana, where he'd been born and raised. With a population of only fifteen thousand, the traffic could never be that bad.

He glanced around the grocery store parking lot, thinking there were probably fifteen thousand people here right now, trying to get something to eat.

Taking a deep breath, he strode over to her window and knocked on it. She shook her head like mad, her short blonde hair flying around that beautiful face. "I just want to ask you something," he said.

"My windows don't roll down," she said, and he could barely hear her through the glass.

"I don't believe that."

"Believe what you want." She didn't try to roll them down, which meant she'd lied to him. Had he really been that rude? She'd almost smashed into his truck, and that, plus his dogs, was all he had left from his almost forty years in Montana.

"Fine," he practically yelled, frustrated at her and hungrier than he'd been in a while. "I have ways of finding out who you are."

That got her to get out of the car, and she almost hit him with the door as it came flying open violently. "Are you threatening me?" she asked, her blue eyes blazing with fire. "I didn't hit you. Go away."

"I just want to know your name."

"Well, too bad. I have no business with you."

"I'll find out." Why he cared, he wasn't sure. Maybe because she was the first person to make him feel alive since the sale of the ranch. And if he were being honest with himself, long before that even.

"What are you going to do?"

"I got your license plate number. I'll make a few phone calls." He had money, and while he'd never had to throw it around to get what he wanted, he could learn. Oh, yes, if there was one thing Carson Chatworth was doing these days, it was learning all kinds of things he'd never thought he'd have to.

He rounded the front of his truck, catching her muttering, "I hate men like you." He paused, wanting to go back and explain that he really wasn't a bad guy. That she stirred something in him, and he simply wanted a way to contact her later. Maybe take her to dinner so they could get to know each other better.

Their eyes met, and something super-charged flowed between them. For him, it was attraction, but for her, he suspected it was being classified as something else entirely. Probably anger.

That pink tint in her cheeks was so sexy, as was that brilliant, blue tank top and the cute little straw hat she wore. Everything about her appealed to him—well, except the glare. He could do without that.

He tipped his hat at her, glanced at her license plate again, and got behind the wheel of his truck. Once he was out of the way, he reached over to the glove box and got out a slip of paper to write down the letters and numbers before he forgot them.

Then he left this grocery store completely. There would be another one not too far away, and Carson needed space to think.

What he really needed was someplace to call home, as he'd been on the road for over two months. Living in hotels and campgrounds was not the life for him, and he'd applied for a couple of jobs in the area, at local ranches and boarding stables. Surely his lifelong ranching skills could get him on somewhere, preferably Last Chance Ranch, which had advertised a cabin to live in as part of the wages.

He got a sandwich and just drove, having nowhere to go until his interview tomorrow. So he'd drive until he got tired of the vibrations of the road beneath him, and then he'd find a hotel.

With something substantial in his stomach, he reflected on the scene in the parking lot. He hadn't sworn at that blonde woman, or really said anything too bad at all. She'd almost rammed into him, and he was merely checking his vehicle. She'd got out to check too.

Feeling okay with his actions, he rolled down his window and let the warm air blow in. His cowboy hat threatened to get blown away, so he took it off. He cast it a glare, like it was responsible for his father's drinking habit and his brother's online poker addiction.

The debts they'd racked up over the years would've taken Carson his entire life to pay back, and he supposed he should be thankful that the Lord had provided him a way to get out from under their actions. Get away from them.

And he *was* grateful for that. But he was also angry and heartbroken that he'd had to sell Cobble Creek Ranch to do it. He'd only known a Montana summer in all of his thirty-eight years of life, and packing everything he owned into the back of this truck and crossing state lines had cost him more than he'd imagined it would.

But Terry hadn't called once since Carson had left, and he supposed he should put that in the blessings column too. If he were counting those at the moment, which he wasn't.

His father hadn't tried to reach him either, and Carson hoped the two of them were still alive. He didn't hate his father and his brother; he just didn't want to be saddled with taking care of his father's failing health when he did nothing to follow the doctor's directions. Nor did he want to watch Terry play games online when he could be working to bring home the money they needed.

"Disabled," fell from his lips, along with a scoff. Terry was not disabled. He just didn't like working.

"Not your problem anymore," Carson said, and he was at least right about that. But the loneliness he'd experienced since leaving behind everything and everyone he'd ever known had hit him hard. Maybe that was why the woman in the parking lot had lit such a reaction in him.

Tired of driving already, he pulled off the highway and used his phone to find a hotel. Calls, texts, and mapping were about all he used his device for, but it was the best one money could buy.

He'd managed to get the family lawyer on his side and together, they'd split the money from the sale of the ranch so that Carson got fifty-one percent, with the other forty-nine being split between Terry and their father.

Didn't matter. Carson had become a billionaire overnight, and while the number was less in Terry's bank account, there were still nine zeroes at the end. Well, there had been when Carson had left the state of Montana. Who knew what his brother had spent in the past ten weeks.

Another problem Carson didn't have to deal with anymore. His money was safe, protected where neither his father nor his brother could ever access it. He'd bought a new truck, and a new hat, and packed Ted and Tony into the back before driving away.

"Time to stop driving away," he told himself as he went inside to see if this hotel would let him have dogs. The dog waste bags on a pole in the middle of the front lawn was encouraging, and sure enough, they gave him a room for the night no problem.

Now he just had to survive another lonely night before his interview. Yes, his two black labs were great company, but they didn't speak English. They couldn't give advice. He did steal comfort from their loyalty and devotion to him, but what he really wanted was a friend.

He wanted to know who that blonde woman was, and how he might be able to see her again. Because if she would just listen to him, he could explain that he hadn't meant anything by asking her if she'd hit his truck. If they could just talk, then maybe he could ask her out. Maybe he wouldn't have to be alone forever.

THE NEXT DAY, he skipped his morning prayers like he'd been doing for months. God had never seemed to hear him in Montana while he pleaded for a solution to their financial problems that would allow him to keep the ranch he'd grown up working. No, every solution required the sale of their generational land, their herd, crops, all of it.

Not wanting to dwell on the negative, he didn't kneel down as soon as he rolled out of bed. And he'd been happier—at least he thought he was. He worked now, thought things through, and went with what his gut told him. He used to think that was God, leading and guiding his life, but now he wasn't so sure.

Maybe God had abandoned him the way his mother had, all those years ago. She'd been the one to teach him how to fold his arms, how to say a prayer, how to look on the sunny side of life. But apparently, even she had a limit, and she'd left his dad and Cobble Creek Ranch when Carson was only twelve years old.

"Two interviews today, guys," he told Ted and Tony, brothers from a litter he'd bred on the ranch. "Let's hope we get one of them, okay? Then we can find a real house to live in." He straightened his hat and grabbed his duffel bag before heading out to the truck with the dogs.

Last Chance Ranch sat a few minutes up a canyon, the ranch on a bluff that overlooked the valley and bordered the Angeles National Forest. It was beautiful land, and he passed a couple of parked cars for sale at the intersection where he turned to go up to the ranch.

A few minutes later, he arrived at the front gate to the ranch, which was being guarded by a legless robot. It looked like it might be a mailbox, but it was in serious need of repair. He eased his truck by it, noticing instantly that this place was in the process of getting cleaned up.

And whoever was doing it, was doing a great job. *And they need help*, he thought as he passed a couple of roads on his left and nothing but farmland on his right. His heart took courage at the familiar sight of a ranch, and he liked the aura of this place immediately.

He pulled into the driveway of the homestead, as a woman named Scarlett Adams had instructed him, and he said to the dogs, "Okay, so I'm going in. You stay here. I'll be back," before facing the house.

His nerves fired on all cylinders as he walked up the sidewalk, noticing the grass had been freshly cut but that the flowerbeds were bare. The scent of cattle and sunshine hung in the air, and there was no better balm to Carson's soul than that.

After knocking on the door, he only had to wait a few seconds for a redhead to open the door. She was pretty, like the blonde, and yet his heart didn't flounce around in his chest like a fish out of water the way it had at the sight of the other woman.

"Hello," he said, smiling at her. "I'm Carson Chatworth." He extended his hand for her to shake, which she did.

"Come on in," she said, falling back and turning as she walked. "I'm Scarlett Adams. I've got my associates with me today." She pointed to a cowboy sitting at the kitchen table, which had been turned to face the door. "Hudson Flannigan. And Adele Woodruff."

Carson almost fell down at the sight of *Adele Woodruff*—the woman who'd almost hit his truck in the parking lot yesterday. Well, now he knew her name, and he hadn't even had to make any phone calls or toss any money around.

Chapter Three

Adele stared at the cowboy walking toward her. She could not believe that it was the same, arrogant fool who'd practically threatened to call the cops on her. *I got your license plate number.*

She hadn't hit his truck, and she'd sat fuming in her car for a good five minutes before she'd tried backing out again. She'd managed to do it without getting another crazy cowboy in her face, and she could *not* believe he was here right now.

What was God trying to do to her? Hadn't she suffered enough already?

"Hello," Carson said to Hudson, his smile perfectly in place. He shook Hudson's hand and then presented his hand to Adele.

She didn't want to make a scene, so she held out her hand and let him pump it. Zillions of butterfly wings burst to life along her skin where he touched, and her eyes met his for a moment as Scarlett sat at the table.

Adele pulled her hand back, shocked—literally—by the physical reaction to Carson. She'd only had this reaction to a man a couple of times in her life—and she'd ended up married to Hank.

"So," Scarlett said, beginning the interview while Adele clenched her arms across her chest. "You worked a ranch in Montana?"

"I owned the ranch," Carson said, his voice full of confidence. Adele couldn't help scoffing, and it was a bit too loud as her best friend turned to look at her. Scarlett's eyes held a question, but Adele wasn't going to answer it right now. She didn't want to answer it ever.

"Why don't you own it now?" Hudson asked, and Adele thought that was a very good question indeed.

"I had to sell it," Carson said. "And I'm looking for a new place to be." His voice held something softer in the words. Something Adele couldn't process fast enough, but something that touched her heart—and that *really* annoyed her.

"Mostly horses?" Scarlett asked.

"Horses, cattle, whatever," Carson answered. "I can clean stalls and do ranch maintenance. I can fix fences, and feed animals, and assess their needs. I know agriculture issues and have managed the farming aspect on a working cattle ranch."

"Finances?" Scarlett asked, scribbling the things he'd

said like she'd go back and read her notes later. No, Adele knew Scarlett, and if Carson could do half the things he'd just said, he'd leave this kitchen with a job.

Her heart couldn't decide which it wanted. Having him here on the ranch every day meant she'd likely have to see him. They'd have to talk about what happened in the parking lot. She'd have to admit that she was just having a bad day, was stressed, and just wanted to come back to her private cabin here on the ranch.

He'd tell her why he was so upset, and why every pair of jeans he wore looked brand new, and why that dimple in his left cheek was so adorable.

"I had an accountant," he said, and she stopped fantasizing about things she had no right to fantasize about. "But I knew what was going on. We met regularly, and I could definitely do that too." He flashed another smile, this time right at Adele, before turning back to Scarlett. "Whatever you need."

Whatever you need.

Adele decided she needed to make a Needs List and hope he'd come knocking, offering her the same thing he'd just offered to Scarlett. She gave herself a little shake. *No, you don't,* she told herself.

She didn't *need* Carson to fulfill her needs. She was doing that all by herself, thank you very much.

"Great." Scarlett reached across the table and shook his hand again. "You're hired. Adele, will you take him over to the Community and let him pick out a cabin?"

Oh, no, This wasn't happening. Adele kicked Scarlett under the table in a not-so-subtle way, because Carson saw everything. She had a distinct feeling that he didn't miss much, and that scared her as much as it excited her.

Scarlett looked at her, dozens of questions in her eyes. "What?"

Adele gave one quick shake of her head, but Carson stood up. She couldn't say anything in front of him anyway. She hadn't told Scarlett about the incident in the parking lot yesterday, and now she'd have to.

Scarlett stood. "Adele will take you over," she said. "I'm assuming you need somewhere to live? We have cabins on-site, and that's part of your pay."

"Sounds great," he said, glancing at Adele and then looking away. Smart man. At least he seemed to be learning quickly.

Adele couldn't see a way out of taking him over to the Community and giving him a tour of the cabins. She'd told her friend that she'd do anything. Clean out stalls. Feed pigs. Whatever it took to earn the money she needed to pay her bills. And she had. For weeks, she had. And for the past few weeks, she'd actually been happier than she'd been in many, many years.

She was not going to let Carson ruin that. So Scarlett would know she didn't like this new hire, Adele glared at her as she led the way to the front door, looking away when Carson stepped between her and Scarlett.

The heat outside hit her in the chest, and she sighed.

"Look," he said, darting down the steps in front of her. "I'm really sorry about yesterday. Honestly, I am."

Adele couldn't have him being nice to her. Then she'd soften, and hold his hand, and start something with him. Because the attraction between them felt magnetic.

No boyfriends on the ranch.

Hadn't she and Scarlett said that?

Yes. Yes, they had.

But she was pretty sure Scarlett had already started something with Hudson. So why couldn't she have a little fun with Carson?

She shoved the thought away, noticing the dogs in the back of his truck. "Black labs?"

"Yes," he said, walking with her as they approached the truck. "Brothers, from my ranch in Montana."

She cut a glance at him out of the corner of her eye. "I used to have a black lab, when I was growing up. His name was Bubba."

"They're great dogs," Carson said, and Adele congratulated herself on having a normal conversation with him. She couldn't believe she'd shared something so personal, though. After all, Bubba held a special place in her heart.

"They'll fit right in here," she said, putting her walls back up. So he was handsome—*gorgeous* was a better word, actually. He smelled amazing—like pine trees and mint. He obviously had money. If she let her defenses down, she'd fall for him faster than she even knew.

"Okay." She exhaled heavily. "Drive me over to the

Community, and I'll show you the cabins." She started around the front of the truck. "This thing has air conditioning, right?"

He chuckled as he got in, saying, "Yes."

Adele disliked trucks in general, because she felt fat and clumsy getting into them. She wasn't sure where to put her foot, and she ended up half-hopping and half-falling into the truck. Carson said nothing; didn't even look at her. But humiliation burned through her, increasing her internal temperature.

"There are thirteen cabins over here," she said, slipping into tour guide mode. "Hudson lives in the back corner, and Sawyer's taken the one at the end here." He turned, and Adele continued with, "All the other cabins are available, and you can choose any one you want."

He drove around the loop in silence, then started around again. He pulled into the driveway right next to Hudson's cabin, and said, "I like neighbors, and the dogs will like the woods here."

"Great," Adele said dryly, already reaching for the door handle. "Okay, I have to—"

"Would you go to lunch with me?" he asked, totally interrupting her.

She swiveled her face toward him, sure he had *not* just asked her out. "No," she said, sliding out of the truck in an ungraceful way. "Welcome to Last Chance Ranch." She slammed the door and walked away, not even giving the dogs a pat the way she wanted to.

ADELE FOUND peace and comfort in the way her knife moved effortlessly through celery, making each piece uniform. Cooking soothed her, and she didn't even mind the clean-up afterward.

She diced onions and celery and added them to the pot already simmering on her single hotplate. The overhead lights made for hot working conditions, but she didn't mind so much.

After stirring the beef together with the vegetables, she then added salt and pepper and garlic salt. With her board clean, she cored her head of cabbage and chopped it up too. That went in the pot. Then chili powder, and water, and a lid.

While that simmered, she cleaned up and opened a few cans, always making sure she worked on the lovely pieces of gray marble she'd found in a thrift store on her way back from cleaning out Hank's storage unit. She'd experimented for a week before getting the lighting settings correct, and sometimes she had to change them depending on where the sun was.

She usually cooked after her long day on the ranch, and the sun wasn't a factor as Gramps's cabin next door took most of the light from the sunset. The thought of Gramps reminded her that she hadn't checked in on him yet that evening. She would when the cabbage patch stew was finished.

Cabbage felt western and rustic, and anyone could make this simple recipe. She pulled out her phone and started typing up a caption for her video—also an acquired skill over the past few months. She'd studied other foodie video accounts and took notes of when they used emojis and when they posted in their stories or how they moved links in and out of their bio.

She was still starting up, but she'd managed to get tagged by a huge account, and her subscribers had skyrocketed in the past week. That fact made a smile touch her face, and Adele held onto it, unsure of when the last time she'd grinned had been.

She hated that she couldn't feel happiness as easily as she once had. But her life was a hundred and eighty degrees away from where it was a year ago, and she was still adjusting. At least that was what she told herself.

Finished with her caption and still waiting for the cabbage to cook, she turned away from the island in the kitchen and wandered to the front door. She'd installed an extra lock just to make sure no one came in while she was cooking.

Adele wasn't sure why, but she didn't want anyone to know about TastySpot or her culinary skills. "Those are still coming along," she told herself. She hadn't gone to culinary school, but the dream lingered on the horizon. There, but always just out of reach.

Once Hank's debts were paid, Adele was going to look into going to classes. She'd looked before, just after Hank's disappearance, and the price tag had convinced her to take the job here at Last Chance Ranch with Scarlett.

So while she was here, she would work hard, both with the goats and on her cooking. But if the time came that she could leave behind mucking out stalls and become a chef, she'd take it. Oh, yes, she'd take any opportunity that came her way.

Chapter Four

Carson got settled into his new cabin easily and quickly. It helped that he didn't own a whole lot. He'd been right about the dogs liking the woods, and they'd disappeared back there while he unpacked his boxes.

He'd stood on the small back porch and whistled. They'd come tearing out of the trees a few moments later, lapped up a quart of water, and now lay panting at his feet on the front porch while he shaped an indistinct piece of wood into something useful.

"Hey," a man said, and Carson glanced up to see the cowboy who'd been in his interview walking toward him, a golden retriever at his side.

Tony whined, but Ted didn't even move. "Wait," he told the dogs. He stood and went down the steps to shake

Hudson's hand again. "Hey. Hope it's okay I chose the place right next door."

"Of course it is." Hudson looked past him to the porch. "Hound's a gentle dog," he said. "They can play."

Carson whistled at his dogs again, and they came bounding down the steps to sniff Hound. "I wasn't sure if I should come back over and get an assignment or what."

"Scarlett hasn't decided yet," Hudson said. "So just get settled, and I'm sure she'll let you know soon enough." He gestured to his house. "Well, I have to get dinner going."

"This place is just getting started, isn't it?" Carson asked.

"Well, kind of," Hudson said. "I just started last week, and Scarlett is trying to get sponsorship with an animal rescue program. So we're getting things cleaned up. Fences fixed. Animals vaccinated. All of it."

"I can do any of that," Carson said.

"I'm sure you can." Hudson flashed him a smile. "I know Scarlett's glad to have you."

"Yeah." Carson put a smile on his face too. "I'm glad to be here." And he was. He liked the sunshine. He liked the smell of this ranch. He liked spending his time whittling and thinking about what his life could be here.

He cleaned up and loaded his dogs in the back of his truck before dinnertime, before heading down the short canyon to get some groceries for the future and something to eat that night.

After unpacking everything in his cabin, he said,

"Come on, guys. Let's go explore a little bit." He left the cabin on foot, his dogs trotting ahead of him and then coming back to circle him.

He looped through the cabins, counting thirteen. Only three were occupied, and his suspicions about this ranch just getting its feet under it were confirmed. Across from the cabins were alfalfa fields, and next to them the homestead. He walked down the road that bordered that, seeing three more cabins. Only two had lights on in the windows, and the one in the middle put off the scent of something savory and delicious.

As he walked past, the door opened, revealing a rectangle of yellow light in the dusk. He was a hundred yards away, but he could tell the woman coming outside was Adele Woodruff. He should just keep walking, but he didn't.

He stopped and watched as she carried something heavy down the steps and went next door. She kicked the door and called, "Gramps, it's Adele." Her voice carried easily in the stillness on the ranch, and a smile started somewhere near his stomach and rose through him.

Gramps opened the door, and Adele said, "Dutch oven short ribs tonight," in a kind voice. He wanted her to speak to him like that, and he watched while she went inside and Gramps closed the door.

He stood there for a moment longer and then continued his solitary walk down the road. On his left, the land continued without restraint, and he could see more

33

lights in the distance. He reached an intersection and saw barns and stables to his left and a long road still in front of him. The road split two pastures, and he found horses in one and llamas in the other.

"Llamas," he said, somewhat in awe. Hudson had mentioned an animal rescue program, and some of these llamas certainly looked a little worse for the wear. Up ahead, he smelled pigs before he saw them, and sure enough, they came into view around the back of a huge hay barn.

He circled back up past the pigs to find several more buildings, all of them dark. There was more to the ranch, but he couldn't tell what in the darkness. Tony and Ted started barking as they passed another road that ran north, but Carson whistled at them to keep them with him.

"Come on, guys," he said. "Let's get home."

Home. What a strange word. He wondered what constituted a home, and if he could make one here at this ranch.

One of his dogs barked again, but it was farther away than he realized. "Ted," he called. "Tony." He whistled, but they did not come running. Suddenly tired, Carson veered down the road and found a parking lot down there, along with a big empty arena. And his dogs, both of them standing near the fence, stretched out to sniff a couple of baby goats.

"Goats." He chuckled as he approached. "Really, guys? We've seen goats and sheep before." Cobble Creek seemed to be a bit like Noah's Ark, and had two of almost everything. Even ferrets, as Terry had three of those as pets.

One of the goats bleated, and Carson said, "All right. Let's go," to Tony and Ted. He started walking across the parking lot when a car came tearing into it, spitting gravel as it came to a stop in front of him.

The headlights blinded him, so he couldn't see who'd gotten out of the car. But he recognized the displeased, furious voice of Adele Woodruff as she demanded, "What are you doing with my goats?"

"Nothing," he said, watching Ted and Tony streak toward her. Their tails wagged, so they weren't worried about her reception of them.

"Nothing?" she repeated, ignoring his dogs. They sniffed her as she strode toward him. "I could hear them bleating from my cabin across the ranch."

"It's dead silent out here," he said. "And your cabin isn't that far away."

She stopped several feet from him, her headlights illuminating her face. "You've been to my cabin?" She folded her arms, a look of pure disgust on her face.

"No, of course not," he said. "I took a walk around the ranch, and I saw you taking dinner to Gramps. Who's Gramps?"

"No one."

"Your goats are fine," he said. "The dogs have been saying hello to all the animals." He gestured for Ted and

Tony to come to his side. "Come on, guys," he said. "Over here." They trotted back to him, and if Adele was impressed with the level of control over his canines, she didn't show it.

He wondered what it would take to impress this woman, and why he wanted to do it so badly. "We're just on our way home."

"Great, you do that. I'm going to check on my goats."

"They're fine," he said as she blew past him.

"I'll be the judge of that." She paused next to him, and they looked at one another. Carson felt like lightning had struck him, and his only thought was to ask her out again.

Don't do it, he told himself, and thankfully his voice had gone on vacation. She stormed away, and he thawed. "I'm sorry," he called after her, only getting silence in return.

―――――――――

THE FOLLOWING MORNING, he still didn't have an assignment on the ranch. His lifelong habit was to get up before the sun and get work done, and while he hadn't been at Cobble Creek for a couple of months now, his internal alarm clock remained.

Dawn found him practically tiptoeing across the lawn behind the homestead, a card pinched between his fingers. An apology card. Surely Adele couldn't continue to be mad at him after three apologies. Could she?

He didn't knock on her door, thinking the hour too early. Instead, he stuck the card between the door and the jamb and practically ran away from the middle cabin behind the homestead. He wasn't sure why this woman called to him so strongly, nor why he felt like he needed her to forgive him for the parking lot incident.

Away from the cabins, he met another man on the road, and he said, "You must be the new guy. I'm Sawyer Smith."

"Carson Chatworth."

Sawyer wore his hair shaved along the bottom, but it looked dark before it disappeared up into his cowboy hat. "Well, I'm headed over to Horse Heaven if you want to tag along."

"I do," Carson practically shouted. He couldn't waste the hours without working, and he needed something to do. And if he could work with horses, even better. So he changed directions and started walking with Sawyer.

"What else do you do here?" he asked.

"I run the horseback riding lessons on the weekends," he said. "Things have been changing a lot, and I'm glad about them. Scarlett really wants this ranch to be something, and she could really use someone like you to help her."

"She hasn't said anything yet."

"She's got a lot on her plate," Sawyer said. "She's basically let me keep doing what I've been doing, but she's asked I make sure all the horses, pigs, and llamas are

37

healthy and their facilities are in top-notch condition. So I've been doing that."

"How long have you been here?" Carson asked.

"About seven years," he said. "Gramps hired me to help with the animals."

There was that Gramps again. "And who's Gramps?"

"Oh, Gramps is Scarlett's grandfather. He owns the ranch. Well, he did. He's signed it over to Scarlett now, but he's lived here with his wife and family for decades."

Carson thought of Adele taking dinner to him last night. "Is his wife...?"

"Oh, she passed away about seven years ago, too. He's been here alone since, trying to take care of over a hundred animals." Sawyer shook his head. "I've done the best I can, but this place is hundreds of acres, with dozens of daily tasks. Scarlett, though, she's dug right in and done whatever she's needed to do."

Sawyer reached the stables and opened the door. "And Adele too. She came with Scarlett, and the two of them have brought new life to the ranch."

"What does Adele do?"

"She works in the stables here, cleaning and refreshing straw. She feeds the dogs with Gramps in the morning and evening. I think she has a soft spot for the old man." Sawyer chuckled as he entered the stables. "But she mostly works with the goats." He pointed to the wall just inside the door. "So we keep track of all the horses here. Scarlett feeds in the morning, but I think Hudson is going to take that over. We have sixteen horses here, and a couple of them are lame. From what I know, this was a rescue ranch before. Some of the animals have been here for years."

"And Scarlett's trying to do that again."

"Yeah." Sawyer sighed and said, "Okay, so today, we're rotating horses from pasture to pasture, and we need to clean the water troughs."

Carson worked with the horses, moving them where he was told. It was easy, soothing work, and he really enjoyed being somewhere that was a bit more mild in temperature than Montana. The winters at Cobble Creek were murder on the soul, and the summers blazed like the devil himself had a vendetta against the state.

But California was breezy, and though it was summertime, it didn't feel like he existed only a few feet from the surface of the sun.

He didn't really need tutoring in how to move horses or clean troughs or feeding schedules, but Sawyer was easy to talk to, and Carson appreciated his kindness.

"So do we just eat on our own for lunch?" Carson asked.

"Yeah," Sawyer said. "Scarlett said she's working on hiring people, but a ranch cook is way down the list."

"Is that a thing?" he asked. "At my ranch in Montana, we used to bring food in sometimes. Or my dad would cook."

"Every day?"

"Oh, no, not every day. Few times a week." For some reason, a bolt of homesickness hit Carson, and he flashed Sawyer a smile. "Well, good thing I bought some groceries then. See you after lunch?"

"Yeah, sure, I'll be working with the cattle. Stop by and grab me on your way over."

"Will do." He touched his hat in good-bye and continued to his cabin, where he let Ted and Tony into the backyard for a bit of playtime. He checked his phone, though he hadn't heard it chime nor felt it buzz.

He'd included his phone number in the card he'd left on Adele's front door, and he'd hoped she'd text him.

"A fool's hope," he muttered to himself as he pulled a pizza out of the freezer and twisted the knob to start preheating the oven. Adele was obviously not interested in him. So why did he keep thinking they could get together?

Chapter Five

Adele worked the flour and other dry ingredients into the wet, liking the smooth texture of cinnamon roll dough. She'd speed up the footage until the video was less than sixty seconds, but she took her time to make sure the dough was exactly right.

It rose in a warm spot in the window while she put butter in a bowl under the mounted camera. Then she used her phone to show putting the butter in the microwave and melting it. She measured out cinnamon and sugar, adding a pinch of nutmeg to make her rolls stand out among the many recipes out there. That, and she made a cream cheese frosting with a bit of orange zest. So it was almost an orange-cinnamon roll.

She put together the frosting under the lights and cameras, still waiting for the dough to rise. It was an astronomical amount of work to make cinnamon rolls, and even more to put the video together in order. Hardly anything was done in sequential order, but all the foodie videos were done that way.

With the frosting finished, she put it in the fridge as her air conditioner seemed to be on the fritz lately. Finally, the dough was ready, and she floured the board and rolled out the dough, spreading the partially melted butter over the rectangle. Then she sprinkled the cinnamon and sugar, as well as dotting the dough with splashes of orange zest.

She rolled the dough and used a piece of unwaxed, unflavored dental floss to cut the rolls into one-inch rolls that she placed precisely on the baking sheet under camera three. Both pans went into the oven, and she started the job of cleaning up.

Bit by bit, piece by piece, she got her kitchen back in order and had just sat down on the couch when someone knocked on her front door. She shot back to her feet, her heart pounding.

"Carson...." She let the word hang there, her fury bubbling up. She'd already gotten his card that morning when she'd left the house to feed the goats. She should've stayed there and worked with them, because some of the babies weren't anywhere close to ready for yoga. But the cinnamon rolls had called to her, and she really wanted it to be her video for tomorrow.

She glanced left and right as if armed guards would burst through the walls, but nothing happened. She went to the door and peered through the peephole, only to find Scarlett standing on the front porch.

"Adele," she called. "Can I come in?"

Adele cracked the door a couple of inches and said, "No. I'm busy."

"Busy?" Scarlett tipped up on her toes to see over Adele's head. She was a bit shorter than Adele, and it annoyed her that Scarlett was trying to snoop inside the cabin through a three-inch gap. "Did you make cinnamon rolls?"

Adele had several minutes left on the timer before the rolls would be done. And she didn't want Scarlett inside for reasons she couldn't articulate. So she opened the door wide enough to get out and onto the porch, bringing it closed behind her. "I don't want to talk about it. You said I'd have my privacy out here."

"From cinnamon rolls?" Scarlett searched her friend's face, and Adele didn't like the questioning in her friend's eyes. "You're acting really weird. Secret baking and what was with all that glaring at Carson the other day?" Scarlett edged back on the porch though it wasn't very big. "And you still won't tell me what you're plotting with the goats."

Adele couldn't tell Scarlett about the goats. She had folders of information in a drawer in the kitchen, but things weren't ready yet. She still had to finish training the goats, and get a budget for yoga mats, and do some more research on prices. She had a very good start on a program the ranch could use to generate income, but she wasn't ready to share yet.

Scarlett sighed—a big, heavy sigh like Adele was being a jerk. And maybe she was. So she lifted her chin and said, "I'm willing to tell you two things. Name them."

Scarlett grinned at her. "One: Carson."

Adele rolled her eyes though her heart started to riot inside her chest. Of course Scarlett would want to know about Carson. "Oh, I met him in town the day before he came up for the interview. He was a real jerk, and I was shocked to see him show up here. That's all."

"Met him in town? You didn't mention that."

"Yeah, well, nothing worth mentioning." Her voice pitched up slightly, and to hide it, Adele crossed her arms too. Maybe Scarlett hadn't noticed. Maybe the thrumming in her pulse didn't mean anything.

"You didn't think an incredibly hot man was worth mentioning?" Scarlett's incredulity wasn't hard to hear.

"Not all of them are," Adele said. "Besides, he doesn't need this job."

"How do you know that? He applied."

"Yeah, because he's homesick and bored." She shook her head, about to reveal something she'd sworn to herself she'd take to the grave. "He sold that ranch in Montana because oil was discovered on it. He has plenty of money."

She hadn't looked him up online because she liked him. Nor because he'd left her a cute card with a cartoon elephant holding a balloon that said "I'm sorry," on it in all lower-case letters. She'd looked him up online because no one—*no one*—had jeans that clean when they worked on a ranch. He had so much money—the ranch had sold for twenty billion—he probably threw away his jeans at the end of every day.

Understanding filled Scarlett's expression. "Oh, so you hate him on principle."

"That's right," Adele said, her eyes widening. "I hate him on principle."

Scarlett's shoulders drooped, and she drew Adele into a hug and said, "I'm sorry it still hurts."

Adele melted into her, her emotions overwhelming her in an instant. Hot tears stung her eyes, and she let a single tremor of grief out. "I hate that it still hurts." She pulled away and wiped her face. "I hate that he still gets to make me feel like this."

Hank. Why did he get to influence her so easily, over a year later? It didn't seem fair, but she kept a tight grip on her emotions and sent a prayer up to the Lord to help her find peace. She'd certainly found more here than anywhere else, and she held that tightly too.

Everything inside Adele was so, so tight.

"It gets better," Scarlett said. "I mean, I know you hate it when I say that, but it's true."

Adele nodded and tucked her hair behind her ear, where it fell right back out again. She hated her hair at this length. "What's the second thing?"

Scarlett looked at the closed front door and back to the

homestead, clearly trying to make a decision. "Goats," she finally said.

Adele breathed a sigh of relief, because she wasn't sure if she could tell Scarlett about the food videos right now. She straightened, ready to put on a professional show. After all, she was going to ask for money too. "Fine, but I don't have all the details worked out yet, so keep that in mind."

"It's in mind."

"Goat yoga." A vein of excitement squirreled through her as she said each word very clearly.

"Goat yoga?" Scarlett laughed, and Adele wanted to stomp back inside and slam the door behind her. Thankfully, Scarlett cut the sound off quickly and asked, "Really, Adele?"

Adele had always thought much farther out of the box than Scarlett. "Really, Scarlett. People are doing all kinds of alternative exercise these days, and yoga is huge. Hot yoga. Beach yoga. And we could do goat yoga. I'm a trained yoga instructor, and we have the facilities. They've been doing it down South for a year or so—I saw it on TV a couple of months back—and I've been training the baby goats."

"Baby goats?"

"Well, you can't have a fifty-pound adult goat jumping on people."

"The goats jump on people?" Her eyes widened, and she shook her head a little. "Adele...."

"No, really." Adele held up one hand like she needed more time to explain, which she did. "I have a whole folder of information on it. The babies only weigh about fifteen pounds or so, and they are so smart. I've been training them with graham crackers, and they let me pick them up. They jump on my back when I'm doing my poses. They're awesome. And—*and.*" She took a deep breath. "We could charge $25 per person for an hour of yoga with the goats. Put up to thirty people in that enclosure we've got out there next to the pens. I've been leveling it and with straw down, it's perfect. The babies are used to being in there, and if we could get the mats, we'd be set to go. Sort of."

Scarlett looked like Adele had hit her with a brick. It was a lot of information, and Adele had been absorbing it, making plans, drawing diagrams, and researching programs for weeks now.

"Sort of?" Scarlett asked.

"Well, I need someone to help me run the program. Maybe a couple of people."

"To do what?"

"While I'm teaching yoga, I'd need at least one person to tend to the goats. Make sure they jump up on every person, circle them through the people. Stuff like that."

Scarlett's smile widened, but it looked more like the Cheshire Cat than anything else. Adele didn't like that. Not one little bit.

"You know who you can have, right?" she asked.

Adele shook her head, horror cascading through her. "No. Scarlett, come on. Give me Hudson."

Scarlett started laughing. "No way. I've already got him making signs. Not only that, but I just assigned him to Horse Heaven, and he still has to fix all those cars." She pushed her flyaways back and sighed. "Jewel Nightingale called a couple of nights ago, and this place has to be *perfect* when she comes. Hudson's helping me with all of that."

"Oh, I bet he is." Adele grinned and lifted her eyebrows.

Scarlett shrugged. "And maybe I like him a little bit."

Adele stared at Scarlett, though she'd suspected her friend and Hudson would end up together. "I thought we weren't doing boyfriends on the ranch."

"Oh, we're not," Scarlett said. "I mean, you hate Carson. So you're safe. *We* aren't doing anything." She moved down the steps, her two questions answered. "Anyway, I stopped by to ask you if you'd talk to Carson about taking over in LlamaLand and Piggy Paradise." At the bottom of the stairs, she turned back and smiled up at her friend. "And now goat yoga too. It sounds like it could really bring in some cash."

"Yeah, about that." Adele skipped down the steps, her heartbeat stumbling over itself too. "I, uh, want half the money. The other half can go to the ranch." She forced herself not to twist her hands, not to blink too much, not to shuffle her feet.

Scarlett cocked her head to the side. "How often are we doing goat yoga?"

"I was thinking every morning and every evening," Adele said. "We're not that far up the canyon, and we might get people who come every day."

"Not for twenty-five dollars a class," Scarlett said.

"So we offer them a monthly fee, the way a gym membership does."

"I'm sure you have all those details in your folder," Scarlett said.

"I'm still working on it," Adele said.

"Talk to Carson," Scarlett said. "And I'd love to see this goat yoga going before Jewel comes out to the ranch. Let's talk again tonight, and I want to see times for the sessions. I'll try to schedule her to come while one is running."

Adele rejoiced inwardly. If she could get goat yoga up and running, she'd have a third income stream, something she desperately needed. "Thanks, Scarlett," she said, keeping her voice as calm and even as possible. "And one more thing."

Scarlett turned back, a flash of impatience on her face. "Yeah?"

"Could you ask Hudson about fixing my car? It has a starter problem."

She grinned and nodded. "That's an easy one. I'll talk to him." She started across the lawn, and Adele waited until she was a good, healthy distance away before she went back up to the door and slipped inside.

The timer on the oven went off only a moment later, and she hurried to get her cinnamon rolls out of the oven before they got too brown.

"WHAT DO YOU THINK, ROCKY?" She held out her fingers for the little brown, white, and black goat, who came trotting over for the treat. Several others followed—Cotton Candy, Cookie Dough, Neapolitan, Praline—but she didn't give out any more graham crackers. The goats would follow anyone with crackers, and surely Carson could put some crumbs in his pocket and circulate the goats through the yoga attendees while she taught.

"Of course he can do it," she told the herd of baby goats. "I just...." She didn't know how to finish that sentence. She didn't want him in her space, with her goats. She'd been working with them since she arrived, the idea for goat yoga coming almost the moment she'd stepped foot into the Goat Grounds.

She'd asked Scarlett for the goats, and her friend had been so consumed with the rest of the problems on the ranch that she'd said yes immediately. She sighed at the thought of sharing her goats with anyone, least of all Carson Chatworth.

But she couldn't resist his good looks and cowboy

charm if they started working together. She knew she couldn't.

She also knew there was no one else on the ranch to help. So she drew in a big breath, said, "All right, guys. Wish me luck," and sighed heavily. She tossed the graham cracker crumbs around the arena and faced the Community, hoping she wouldn't have to traipse all over the ranch to find Carson.

Chapter Six

Carson pulled the pizza out of the oven amidst a huge plume of smoke. He coughed and practically threw the baking sheet on top of the stove. A slam got the oven shut, and he flipped the knob back to zero.

Someone knocked on the front door. He spun toward it, his heart already bouncing around near the back of his throat. Maybe it had been the oven. Or the baking sheet cooling and unwarping.

Because another look at it, and it was definitely not flat anymore. He'd made frozen pizza before—he wasn't completely unable to feed himself—but he'd never had smoke come out of the oven after only ten minutes.

He coughed again, sure his lungs were getting infected by some sort of toxic fumes. That oven was unusable. He didn't dare open it, but once it cooled, he'd see if a vat of sludge had spilled inside.

"Carson," a woman called, and he strode toward the door to open it. Ted and Tony escaped outside, leaving Carson to face their visitor. Adele stood there, looking glorious and glamorous in a pair of skin-tight jeans, a white blouse that looked like it had fallen into a washing machine full of bleach, and a black vest.

His mouth went dry.

"Everything okay in there?" She waved her hand in front of her face.

"So my oven has something spilled inside it," he said, easing out onto the porch with her. "And I just tried to make pizza. So it's a little smoky."

"A little smoky?" She half-choked, half-coughed. "I'm dying."

"Let's go to lunch," he said, seizing the opportunity.

"Very funny," she said. "I just came by because Scarlett asked me to let you know your ranch assignments."

Finally, he thought but kept buried under his tongue. He might be new to the dating scene, but he understood female friendships. And Adele and Scarlett were obviously very close. He wiped his hands down the front of his jeans, surprised to find Adele staring at his legs after he finished.

"All right," he said, jerking her attention back to him.

"All right," she repeated, those clear, blue eyes soaking him up. He wasn't sure if he should smile or just stand there. He chose to stare back, if only to give her some of her own medicine. "Are you going to tell me my ranch assignments, or am I supposed to read your mind?"

She blinked, the fire coming back into her gaze a moment later. He wasn't sure which he liked better—the softer version of her or the don't-mess-with-me blonde he'd met a couple of days ago in a parking lot.

"She wants you in LlamaLand and Piggy Paradise." She cleared her throat and fell back a step. "And the goal grinds." She practically whispered the last few words, and Carson didn't understand her.

"And what?" He squinted at her. "The goal grinds. What's that?" Coal? Was there coal on this ranch?

Sparks flew from Adele's eyes, but they only served to fuel the flame of desire already burning in Carson's chest. "The Goat. Grounds." She enunciated each word clearly this time, in a loud voice.

"Don't you work with the goats?"

"Yes." She folded her arms and leaned in. "How did you know that?"

"Besides you practically running me over the other night? Sawyer told me."

She had nothing to say to that, and he really wanted to ask her if she'd gotten his card. Instead, he stood there, his stomach growling and his lungs continually breathing in and out. Adele didn't say anything or move to leave. He had no idea what kind of game this was, but he liked playing it with her.

After one particularly loud grumble from his stomach, she said, "I have some leftovers you can have for lunch."

Shock hit him hard, almost physically knocking him backward. "Really, Adele? That would be great. Thanks."

She put her hand flat against his chest and pushed. The warmth from her hand seeped into his skin, and shivers erupted up and down his arms. He held very, very still so she wouldn't know how strongly she affected him.

"You can *not* come inside my house. It's non-negotiable."

"Okay," he said when he really wanted to ask, *Why not?* "Is there a dead body in there?" he joked.

"Yes," she said without so much as a twitch of her lips. "Yours, if you even attempt to come inside. *I* will go in and get you something to eat. You can wait on the porch. The end. Those are the terms."

"Terms?" Carson scoffed, realizing a half a second too late that it was the entirely wrong thing to do. "Yes, fine. I agree to the terms." If he could spend ten minutes walking with her back to her cabin, Carson thought he might sign away a kidney.

"Fine, let's go. I'll fill you in on the goats on the way." She turned and started down the steps.

Carson hurried to follow her, whistling for his dogs. "Just a sec. I gotta put Tony and Ted back in the house."

"Oh, they can come," she said. "I love dogs."

"Will you let them inside the house?" he asked.

"No," she said.

"Does Gramps get to go inside your house?"

"No."

"Scarlett?"

She sighed, stopped walking, and faced him. "No, Carson. No one goes inside my house." She started striding forward again, and for someone who was several inches shorter than him, she sure could move fast.

"I know a little bit about goats," he said when he caught up to her again. "We had five or six on the ranch in Montana."

"These goats are completely different."

"How do you know?"

"I just do. We have miniature Norwegian goats, and I need your help with the goat yoga program I'm starting, not in caring for them."

Carson frowned, trying to put her words into an order that made sense. "Goat...yoga?"

"Yes."

"I'm afraid I am unfamiliar with that."

She cut him a look out of the corner of her eye, and he thought he saw a smile. It was there for a moment, maybe a breath, maybe a step, and then gone. "Most people are. Don't worry, I have a folder of information I can give you. And we'll head over to the arena when we're done with lunch."

Carson wanted details now, from her mouth, if only to keep her talking to him in such a civilized manner. He liked the sound of her voice, and walking next to her, and the scent of cinnamon and sugar that swirled around her.

But he kept his mouth shut, because he sure did like the sound of *we* coming from her as well. They reached the end of the road with all the cabins, and he asked, "Are you going to eat with me?"

"Believe it or not, I eat lunch too," she said.

"Well, yeah, of course. I just wondered if...I can't come inside, will you stay outside and eat with me?"

Another look out of the side of her eye. Another almost-smile. How had this woman wrangled his heart so quickly? And without even being nice to him.

"Depends," she said.

"On what?"

"How much you annoy me between now and my place. And I gotta say, cowboy, you're already at about a seven."

"Out of what?" Wow, he liked hearing her call him a cowboy.

"Seven." She laughed then, and he wondered if this was flirting.

"All right, all right," he said. "Shutting up now."

"You don't have to shut up," she said. "You just have to say things that don't irritate me."

"Like what?"

"Oh, I don't know. Siblings?"

"Yeah, well, those annoy me," he said darkly. "Pass. What else?" He caught a look of interest from her, but he really wasn't up for explaining about his brother and his online poker addiction. Nor his sister-in-law, if Tammy could even be called that. She only came out to the ranch when she wanted...favors from Terry, and their marriage was only on paper.

Carson wanted so much more than that, and his hand twitched toward Adele's like he might hold it. *Nope*, he commanded himself. She would not like that, as evidenced by how she'd reacted when he'd grabbed her arm the other day.

"How do you like California?" she asked.

"It's great," he said. "The climate is so much more mild than Montana." He wanted to kick a hole in the ground and bury himself. The weather? Was he really talking about the weather with this gorgeous woman?

He swallowed and reminded himself that he'd had girlfriends before. Sure, only a few, and not one for a couple of years. But still. He had money, and knowledge, and a good work ethic. There was no reason Adele couldn't like him.

"Have you always lived here?" he asked.

"In California, yes," she said. "I grew up in Crystal Cove."

"Oh," he said. "Nice."

"You've never been there, have you?"

"No, ma'am. But the list of places I've never been is quite long." Carson didn't feel bad saying it. He was full of country, and he didn't mind that he'd lived in Montana for his whole life.

"Well, maybe now that you're rich, you should travel the world."

Carson almost tripped over the tips of his boots. "Now that I'm rich?" He tried to watch her and the ground simultaneously, because he didn't want to miss her reaction to his question, but he really didn't want to trip and fall flat on his face either.

"I mean—"

"How do you know I'm rich?"

She didn't speak for a few seconds, and she strategically kept her face turned away from him, as if watching hay grow was the most fascinating thing on the planet.

"Your jeans are never dirty," she said.

Confusion riddled his mind. "What?"

"Cowboys should have dirty jeans. Unless they're cowboy billionaires. Then they have so much money, they can buy three hundred and sixty-five pairs of jeans and always have a clean pair."

Carson opened his mouth to say something, but honestly, nothing came to mind. Not a single thing. Much like she didn't want anyone in her house, he didn't want to discuss his finances with a single soul.

He said, "Well, at least now I know what your qualifications are for a billionaire."

She made a noise kind of like a scoff or a choke, and Carson looked at her again. "Are you *laughing*?" he asked.

She shook her head, but the smile stayed on her face, and the rusty laughing kept spilling from between those full lips. They crossed the lawn, and she went up the steps of the middle cabin.

Carson stayed on the grass and looked up at her from beneath the brim of his cowboy hat. "I'll stay right here."

"I'm not a savage," she said. "You can sit on the steps after I go in." She flashed another quick smile and turned to open the door. "Wait." She turned back. "What do you want? Soup? Casserole? Chicken breast?"

"You've got all of that as leftovers?"

"I make dinner every night," she said, a hint of something false in her voice. So Adele Woodruff wasn't a great liar.

"I don't care," he said. "Surprise me." He was already past surprised she'd offered him lunch. That she'd laughed. And she'd obviously looked him up somehow, because his jeans weren't brand new.

She went inside, and he glanced down at his jeans. They were definitely dirty from his morning in the stables and pastures, and if she couldn't see that, maybe she needed an eye exam. He sat down on the top step and faced the homestead, a sense of peace descending on him. He'd felt like this at Cobble Creek too, and he loved the sound of silence in the country, the distant hum of a machine working somewhere on the ranch, and the far-away barking of dogs.

Dogs.

His adrenaline spiked when he remembered Ted and Tony, and he whistled, loud and long. His black labs came running from the hay fields, and they came right up on the steps with him.

"Hey, fellas," he said, rubbing each one with one of his hands. "What are you doin' out there in the hay, huh? You leave that alone."

The door behind him opened, and he turned to see Adele carrying a serving platter the way butlers did in movies. "Let me help," he said, shoving his dogs away and getting to his feet while she was still trying to balance the tray and close the door.

Smartly, he took the tray from her and let her lock up her cabin. Then they sat on the top step together, and Carson banished Ted and Tony to the lawn and told them to stay.

"This smells great," he said, taking in the spread on the tray now balanced on his knees. "Stew?"

"Cowboy stew," she said. "It's mostly ground beef and cabbage, with some beans and corn."

"Did you make these cinnamon rolls?"

"This morning."

"No wonder you smell so sweet," he said, reaching for one of the cinnamon rolls first.

"Is that a pick-up line?" she asked, and Carson looked at her.

"No, ma'am. You smell like cinnamon and sugar. I noticed it on the way over."

She ran her hand from the top of her head to the ends of her short hair. She tucked it behind her ear, but it sprang right back out.

"Is this the goat yoga folder?" he asked when he started taking plates and bowls off the tray and saw the manila folder.

"Yep."

"Can we eat first? I'm starving." He slid the tray to her, with just her soup and cinnamon bun on it. Then he plucked the folder from the tray and set it next to him on the steps. He tore off a piece of cinnamon roll, noting how tender and soft it was. The flavor of sugar, cream cheese, cinnamon, and orange exploded in his mouth, and he groaned.

"Holy brown cows, Adele," he said. "What are you doing on this ranch? You should be a chef."

Chapter Seven

"I want to be," Adele said without censoring herself.

"Yeah?" he asked, his mouth still partially full of cinnamon roll. "This is the best thing I've ever put in my mouth."

"Thank you," she said, suddenly feeling more melancholy than she wanted to admit—or show to Carson. She felt like she was losing her mind. First, she'd invited him to her cabin for lunch. No, not inside it. But still. She'd shown interest in him. Second, she'd asked him personal questions about himself.

He wouldn't talk about his family, and that had lifted her curiosity to astronomical levels. And now she was telling him personal things about herself.

"So what are you doing on this ranch?" he asked, dipping his spoon into the soup.

"Scarlett's my best friend. She needed help, and I needed a job."

"So you're not a chef." He wasn't really asking, but he was eating the soup at the speed of light.

Adele picked up her spoon and took a bite too, buying herself some time to answer him. The soup was spicy and sweet, savory and warm in her mouth and stomach. She took a few more bites and said, "Culinary school is expensive."

"Mm," he said.

"And I'm forty-three-years-old," she said. "It feels like I missed my chance."

"Aw, that's not true," he said, still not looking at her. "Look at me. I'm thirty-eight, and I just sold the only ranch and home I've ever known. If this old cowboy can learn new tricks, you can go to culinary school." He nudged her with his elbow, and Adele smiled at him.

It was easier to smile than tell the truth. He didn't want to hear about Hank anyway. She didn't want to detail the hundreds of thousands of dollars she owed because of her ex-husband.

"Have you always worked a ranch?" he asked, looking at her with those blue-green eyes. She'd never noticed what color they were, as she'd always interacted with him through the red haze of anger.

"No," she said. "I was a yoga instructor and a massage therapist in another life."

He didn't miss a beat before saying, "I've got this *really* tight spot on my shoulder here." He turned his back toward her. "It could use the touch of a good masseuse."

"Nice try," she said, but she couldn't help smiling.

"If I paid you, would you rub it out?"

"No," she said.

"Why not?" He gazed at her evenly, not a speck of malice or teasing in his tone.

So she couldn't tell him if she put her hands on him, she'd want to kiss him. "I don't do that anymore," she said.

"But you're going to do the yoga."

"Goat yoga," she corrected. "And you should look at that folder."

"Am I going to need a massage after the goat yoga?"

She giggled—*giggled*—and shrugged. "With your big old shoulders? Probably, especially if that one is already sore."

He picked up the folder, a goofy grin on his face that made him twice as good-looking as he already was. "Let's see what we've got here."

Adele looked away while he scanned several week's worth of her hard work. She needed to show it all to Scarlett too, but she was hoping she and Carson could do that together. Sort of like a united front.

A few minutes later, he closed the folder and picked up the very middle of his cinnamon roll. He'd saved the best bite for last, and Adele had to appreciate that.

"So let me get this straight," he said after he'd swallowed. 'You're going to charge people twenty-five dollars to come to the ranch, go into a pen with thirteen baby goats, and do yoga."

"Yes," she said.

"For an hour."

"Well, the yoga is only forty-five minutes," she said. "Then there's a fifteen-minute Q&A, picture opportunities, and goat petting."

"Goat petting," he repeated. "And you'll be doing the yoga with people."

"Yep."

"And I'll be...."

"The goat wrangler," she said. "You'll get the goats out of their pens and into the arena. You'll put the goats away. You'll keep an eye on all the goats during the session, you know, make sure people aren't misbehaving."

"The people aren't misbehaving."

"Oh, the goats know exactly what to do," she said. "And you'll be walking around the group, so that everyone gets an authentic goat yoga experience. The babies love graham crackers, and you'll just keep some of those with you. You'll be like the Pied Piper, but with goats." She looked at him, expecting him to laugh. He didn't.

Instead, he looked at the closed folder and back to her. "I want to see the goats."

"Just waiting on you, cowboy."

He smiled as he stacked his dishes and put them on the tray. He courteously kept his back to her as she edged inside her cabin, and then they set off across the lawn again, the folder of information tucked under his far arm.

"Are you skeptical?" she asked. "I have videos I can show you."

"Skeptical is a good word," he said. "But you know what, Adele? I don't know you all that well, but you seem like a smart woman to me."

She glowed with warmth with his compliment, and her fingers brushed his when she stepped. Every cell in her body twittered at her, and when they stepped again, she laced her fingers through his. "Thank you, Carson." She squeezed once and let go of his hand, her own burning with the touch of him.

He exhaled slowly, and she wondered what that was about. She didn't want to ask, so she kept her mouth shut except to say, "I named all the goats when I got here. Gramps said none of the animals had names, except the dogs. So that was one of the first things Scarlett and I did."

"Hmm."

"The adult goats are named after candy bars," she said. "And the babies are after ice cream flavors."

He chuckled, the sound deep and rich and floating on the air between them. "Which one's your favorite?"

"Rocky Road."

"The goat or the flavor?"

"Both," she said. "What about you?"

"Well, I haven't met the goats yet, but I'm partial to lime sherbet."

Her heart fell right through her ribs. "I didn't name a goat that." And Sherbet was a great name for a goat. What had she been thinking?

His aquamarine eyes practically sparkled at her from underneath that hat. "That's too bad. Guess we'll have to go to town and get ice cream then."

Adele didn't say no, though the word teemed just below her tongue. She didn't say yes either, but instead opened the gate to the arena and went in before him. He followed, closing the gate behind him like a true cowboy would.

"This is where the yoga will take place," she said. "I've almost got it leveled, and I'm bringing in straw. I need to meet with Scarlett, and we'll get yoga mats. After that, it's just goats, people, and graham crackers that we need."

"They really like graham crackers?" He shoved his hands in his pockets and looked around.

"Yes." She walked along the back fence. "The goats are kept here during the night, and I let them out to graze during the day." She opened another gate and went through it. "They've got outdoor arenas here, and a barn with stalls."

"How many goats do you have total?"

"Um, thirty-four?" Adele thought out loud when she continued with, "Thirteen babies, and twenty-one adults. That's thirty-four."

"Yes, it is." Carson moved forward and leaned against the fence. "They're out to pasture?"

"With the cattle," she said. "Which you're in charge of too, by the way," she said. "I think I forgot to mention that."

He looked at her for a long moment, and Adele thought she might be able to dive right into those eyes.

"So." She cleared her throat and walked toward the door that led into the barn. "Do you want to see them in action?"

"The goats?"

"Yes, the goats." She took a package of graham crackers from the shelf and handed them to him. "Small pieces. And they have to jump on me before they get one. Jump and stay for a few seconds. They can't just jump up and get down right away."

"So you're training them like dogs."

"Yes," she said. "Exactly like that."

He followed her through the barn and into a pasture, the nearness of him throwing her out of equilibrium. Before she'd met him, she'd known exactly what she wanted: Pay off her debts and go to culinary school. She still wanted those things, but now she was mentally trying to calculate how to include him in her plans.

Which made absolutely no sense. She'd known him for three days now, and seventy-five percent of that time, she'd been annoyed by him.

"Hey, babies," she cooed to the goats who were clustered right by the gate. She counted them quickly, asking, "Where's Vanilla?" before glancing out further into the pasture. The small white goat came trotting as quickly as she could, but she was on the small side and had obviously been further out than the other goats.

"Come on," she said. "We have to show this cowboy how we can jump up." She opened the gate and ushered them into the outer pen, then walked around it to a gate she'd had Sawyer put in last week.

She pointed to it. "You open this one," she said. "Give me one of those crackers."

He complied, and she walked over to the gate that would take them into the yoga arena. "All right." She held up the cracker while he opened the gate, and all thirteen baby goats made a beeline for her.

Pride filled her chest, and she couldn't help grinning at her little goats. Then Carson. "All right, cowboy. Come watch this." She entered the arena after the goats, breaking off pieces of cracker and treating all of them while murmuring praises at them.

She spread a thick blanket on the ground and got down on her hands and knees. Foolishness blipped through her—until a goat jumped right up on her back.

"Good," she said. "Carson, you treat him. Then tell him to get down."

Carson hurried over and did as she said, and almost instantly, another goat jumped on her back. She laughed, and while sometimes the hooves pressed on a tender area, for the most part, the babies were light enough for a person to handle.

She changed positions, lifting a leg or an arm, doing some lower back stretches, whatever she could to tilt her body and still get a goat to balance on her.

When all thirteen had demonstrated their abilities, she got up and brushed off her jeans. "See?"

Carson gaped at her, wonder in his eyes. The graham cracker package was still almost full, and he looked from it to the goats to her. Then he swept her right into his arms. For one terrifying moment, she thought he'd kiss her. But he simply held her close to him, and it was glorious and wonderful.

He released her as quickly as he'd embraced her. "That was phenomenal," he said, a little breathlessly. "I mean, it was awesome. They did great." He bent down and patted Mint Chocolate Chip, a huge grin on his face. "Will they jump on me?"

"They better," she said. "Get down there, cowboy. Don't be afraid to get those jeans dirty."

"No problem," he said with a mischievous twinkle in his eye. "I'll just throw these out and get a new pair out for tomorrow."

She couldn't help laughing with him, and he made getting down on his hands and knees look like the sexiest move a man could make. Minty jumped on him in the next moment and looked at Adele as if to say, "Treat now, please."

She gave him a bit of cracker and pointed to the ground. Minty didn't get off right away, but turned in a full circle on Carson's back, which caused him to groan as he laughed. Adele beamed at the goat, treated him again, and pointed to the ground.

He got down, and another goat jumped up. "This is Cookie Dough," she said. "Female goat. About nine pounds."

"She feels like ninety pounds on my back."

"Oh, you're such a big baby." Adele laughed as Carson went down on his elbows and another goat—Strawberry—leapt up on him, spun, and got down, all before Adele would give her a cracker.

He laughed as he got up and dusted off his hands and knees. "That was great, Adele. I can't wait to see if people here will take to this."

"I think they will," she said, her nerves suddenly firing. She needed them to. She could make four hundred dollars per session if she could fill them. Scarlett's part of the money would go to maintaining the goats, caring for them, providing food and medical attention. And Adele's earnings would go a long way toward saving for culinary school.

"My market research suggests people will go crazy for this."

"When does it start?" he asked.

"I'm thinking a couple of weeks," she said. "On a Saturday morning. I need to meet with Scarlett, and then maybe you and I can work together to prepare the marketing materials."

"Sure," he said easily, still fixated on the goats.

"See?" she said. "People like them. Even you like them."

"I do," he said, lifting his eyes to hers. "I really do like them."

Adele ducked her head, because it felt like he was saying more than what he'd actually articulated. Feeling brave and bold when her stomach was really quaking, she linked her arm through his and plucked a graham cracker from the package.

"All right, enough for one day. Have you seen the Canine Club yet? Ted and Tony would love it there."

Chapter Eight

Carson woke for a few mornings in a row, his memories of the day before full of Adele's perfume, her curvy legs as she did yoga poses and called to him to move around her and through the goats to make sure they all could jump up and down off a person, and no fighting.

They hadn't been fighting, and he smiled on Friday morning as he got up and stepped into the shower. As he brewed coffee and put an English muffin in the toaster. As he delivered Ted and Tony to the Canine Club, where they'd been spending their days with other dogs.

Adele had been right—his dogs did love the big open space with trees, places to dig, and other dogs.

Carson spent his mornings with pigs, llamas, and horses, and his afternoons with Adele. It was the best way to end a day that he'd ever had, and he didn't mind the time he spent on the ranch before lunch either.

He went out onto the porch, the clear day ahead of him holding more hope than he'd experienced in a long time. For a moment, he let his eyes drift upward, as if he'd give the glory of the day to God.

His phone went off as he walked down the road, his two dogs at his side. A smile lit his whole being when he saw Adele's name on his screen. She'd never texted before lunchtime, and he read her message quickly.

Come to the homestead as quickly as you can. Our Saturday session is full already!

"Full already?" Carson looked up as if the people who'd bought a ticket to their first goat yoga session would already be at the ranch, suited up in spandex, and ready to begin.

He increased his pace, deciding to take his dogs with him to the homestead first. Last night, he'd spent a couple of hours with Adele—on her steps—going over her marketing plan and how to get the word out. He'd checked and double-checked her sign-up form to make sure the automation worked and customers got their tickets emailed to them immediately upon purchase.

And together, they'd made the Last Chance Ranch website live, posted on Facebook, and been reassured via text that their flyers were up in the grocery stores and would go out in various emails for local attractions the next morning.

This morning.

Like, an hour ago.

And they'd filled their first session already? He jogged across the lawn, his dogs thinking he was going to give them an adventure. As he took the stairs up to the front door, he heard feminine laughter and figured it was safe to go inside without knocking.

He did, only to find Scarlett and Adele bouncing up and down as they laughed. He watched them for a moment, their joy radiating through him. Then he cleared his throat, and Adele's eyes moved to him.

She sobered quickly, and said, "So we'd like to go over a few logistics." Pure professionalism resided in her voice. "Do you have a few minutes?" She looked into the kitchen, where Hudson stood. Carson hadn't even seen him, as he only seemed to have eyes for the curvy blonde in front of him.

"Yeah, sure," Scarlett said, glancing at Hudson too. "Hudson and I can chat later."

The other cowboy watched Scarlett for another moment, then nodded and touched the brim of his cowboy hat before moving toward Carson. "Hey, Carson," he said as he brushed past, and Carson got the distinct impression that he and Adele had just interrupted something between Hudson and Scarlett.

"Okay, so like I said, our first session next Saturday is sold out. That evening class went next, and then the morning sessions started filling. I was watching on the computer, and we got eleven people to sign up for once a week classes in the first thirty minutes." Adele spoke as if she'd just gotten everything she wanted for Christmas, her exuberance and excitement contagious as she had Scarlett pull up the website she'd put together herself.

"It's not perfect," she said. "But it gets the job done. Carson helped me find the back-end plug-ins we needed for commerce." She flicked her gaze at him and then focused back on the screen.

"The money goes into an account I set up on Wednesday morning, and we've never talked about how to pay the ranch."

"I have a business account too," Scarlett said. "You can just transfer it to that, right?"

"I'm sure we can." Adele looked at Carson again.

"We can write you a check," Carson said, wondering when he'd become a partner in the goat yoga operation. "Or pay through electronic payment using your email address."

"Let's just do that," Scarlett said.

"Tell me the email you want me to send it to," Carson said. "We'll pay...what, Adele? End of every week? Every month?"

They both looked at Scarlett, who wore an equally blank look on her face. "Whatever works for you guys," she said.

"I'll decide," Carson said, giving a nod to Adele.

"And how will the class work again?" Scarlett asked, and Adele started detailing how the sessions were broken down, how good the goats were getting, and how their social media accounts were going to explode once the classes actually started.

"So I need to keep posting," she said. "Our Facebook and Instagram is so new." She looked at Carson with worry in her eyes.

"Well, you're good at that," Scarlett said. "I mean, your—"

"Sh," Adele said, much too loudly and for far too long. She stared at Scarlett and then briefly met Carson's eyes.

The meeting wrapped up a few minutes later, and Carson left through the back door with Adele. He wanted to wake up in the morning fight-free, but he also wanted to know more about her.

"What was she going to say back there?" he asked, pausing on the lawn so when Adele kept walking, she wouldn't be able to reach him.

"About what?" she asked.

"When she said you were good at social media."

She paused too and turned around. He caught the tail-end of her eyeroll. "My first husband worked in Hollywood," she said. "I got very good at managing his social media presence."

Carson's eyebrows went up. "First husband? So you've been married before."

"That's right." Adele paced back toward him. "Is that a problem for you?"

"Not at all," he said, wondering why it would be a problem for him. Did she think...well, what did she think? They worked together, and he hadn't been shy about asking her out. She still hadn't accepted though.

Something pulsed between them, and she asked, "What about you? Ever been married?"

"No, ma'am." He instinctively touched the brim of his cowboy hat and glanced down. "I, uh, didn't even date that much in Montana. The ranch was kind of isolated."

A charged sparkle entered her eyes, and she took a slow step forward. "A handsome cowboy like you didn't date?" She grinned at him and reached up to touch his cowboy hat right where he had.

A flare moved through him though she hadn't even touched him.

"See you after lunch," she said, taking a couple of steps backward before turning and walking away from him. He watched her go, his blood running hotter with every sway of her hips.

SUNDAY MORNING FOUND Carson frowning at his phone. Adele had invited him to church.

Church.

Carson had been sitting on the front porch with a

carving knife in his hand, and the piece he'd been whittling had lost its shape the moment he'd read her question.
The war inside him continued to rage, and he still hadn't
answered her.

Hudson came out of his cabin and got in his truck,
wearing a pair of black slacks, a white shirt, and a gray and
purple tie. So he was going to church too. He didn't see
Carson on the porch, but Carson watched until his truck
couldn't be heard or seen anymore. Several minutes later,
his truck rumbled past the turn-off into the Community,
and Carson got the very real feeling that he'd just been left
on the ranch alone.

Sure enough, Adele's next text said, *Didn't hear from
you. I'm making lunch after church if you want to come.*

He couldn't answer right away, because he didn't want
her to know he'd seen her earlier text and ignored it. He
hadn't really ignored it. He hadn't known how to respond.
He wanted to spend time with her. He just didn't want to
do it in a church.

The guilt threading through him stung, just like he
expected it to. He set down the knife and tossed the
useless piece of wood. "Come on Teddy," he said to his
dog. "Tony, let's go for a walk."

He had to get away from his house for a bit, and this
ranch was huge. Hudson had asked him to go on some
mapping expeditions, and Carson had readily agreed. He
walked with the dogs over to the stables, saddled Moonbeam, a pretty black horse with a splash of white across

83

her back, and set out with the sunshine as an additional companion. The fresh air had always cleared his mind, and today was no different.

Problem was, with his mind clear, new thoughts found a place inside his head. And today, all he could think about was Adele, the goats, and why he didn't want to go to church. He pulled out his phone and sent a quick message back to Adele.

Lunch would be great.

Maybe if he didn't say anything about church, he wouldn't have to sort through the tangle of feelings inside him regarding his religion. But if it mattered to Adele at all, Carson knew he'd have to explain eventually.

She'd mentioned she was from Georgia, and he didn't know a whole lot about the South—other than they took their religions seriously. He'd wanted to ask her what had brought her to California, but the conversation had moved to something else quickly, and he didn't want to seem too interested in her.

A handsome cowboy like you.

Her words from the other day vibrated through his mind. Maybe it didn't matter if she knew he was interested in her—because he was. And it might be possible that she was interested in him too.

He let Moonbeam plod along, and he didn't take any notes of where he saw things on the ranch. Hudson was doing all of that, and Carson just went along for an extra set of eyes.

"What do you think, Moonbeam?" he asked the horse, and she lifted her head a few inches. "Should I ask Adele out again? Maybe she'd say yes this time."

Moonbeam gave a little whinny, and it almost sounded like she'd said, "Maybe."

Chapter Nine

Adele sat beside Scarlett in the chapel, but her mind wandered along unknown paths on the ranch. Carson hadn't texted until church had already started, but she'd fired off a quick invitation to lunch, and he'd confirmed.

The buzzing in her bloodstream had nothing to do with the sermon, and she couldn't focus for more than two seconds. She had found a nice cut of brisket at the grocery store, and she'd done a video on all the prep for it already this morning.

She'd invited Scarlett and Hudson and Gramps, and it wasn't until she'd announced she'd be making some of her famous—well, back home in Savannah-famous—Southern barbecue that she'd realized they'd be coming to her house.

Her *house.*

She didn't let anyone in her house. So the thoughts

rotated and gnawed their way through her mind, first along the lines of wondering if she could get all the lights and camera equipment down and hidden in her bedroom.

Then she'd remember how long it had taken her to get them mounted, how she'd sliced her finger on the wire pot rack, and how she'd tweaked the cameras for two weeks before she had all the angles right and knew where to put her pots and dishes.

She couldn't take down the equipment. And she couldn't tell anyone about her food videos. She wasn't sure why, but she wanted to hold onto the secret a little bit longer.

She leaned over to Scarlett. "Can we eat at your place?"

Scarlett looked at her, blinking a few times as if to clear her mind so there was room for Adele's question. "What?"

"For lunch," she said. "My...air conditioning isn't working all that well."

"Sure," Scarlett said, and she practically snuggled into Hudson's side.

Adele went back to obsessing over Carson, and if she shouldn't have invited him to lunch. But she wanted to see him today, and he obviously wasn't terribly interested in attending church.

Besides, Carson had asked her out a couple of times, and she wanted to go, especially the more time she spent with him. He had a gentle touch with the goats—and with her. He possessed a calm demeanor, and she felt better with him and after she'd spent time with him than she had in a very long time.

Her grip on her phone tightened, and she once again tried to focus on what Pastor Williams was saying. She'd grown up with a religious mother and father, and she did enjoy the peace that came when she attended church services.

The problem was, she didn't know how to hold onto that peace for longer than a few hours after church. And she really wanted more of it in her life.

As she listened, she realized that the only time she felt that calm reassurance in her life was when she was making her videos. She'd wanted to be a chef for so long, and maybe she should just take the leap, get a loan, and go to culinary school. If she waited until she had enough money to afford the tuition, she'd never go. Hank's debts would keep her paying for years and years, and she was already forty-three-years-old.

Familiar desperation rose in her throat, and she couldn't swallow it away no matter how hard she tried. The hymn started, and she scrambled to her feet to add her voice to the chorus. She enjoyed the ebb and flow of the music as it moved through her, and the tune stayed with her as she filed out of the chapel behind Hudson and Scarlett.

She laced her arm through Gramps's as they crossed

the parking lot to Hudson's truck. "Did you like the service, Gramps?" she asked.

"Oh, yes," he said. "Pastor Williams used to bring my wife the best peach preserves in the world."

"Really?" Adele asked, though Gramps had told her about the peach preserves a few times now. She smiled at him. "Your wife used to put them on graham crackers." In fact, his stories of his wife had inspired Adele to try the sweet, crunchy snacks with the goats.

"Yes," Gramps said. "I think I'll have that for lunch when we get back."

"Oh, I'm making lunch today," she said. "Remember?"

"Yes, yes. Lunch with you." She helped him into the truck and settled beside him in the back seat. The short ride up the canyon brought them to the robot mailbox that Scarlett loved so much and had told her all about.

It was still in disarray, but Hudson had promised to have it ready before the Forever Friends team came to the ranch. He passed the turn-off toward the Community, and Adele employed all of her willpower to keep from looking down that way to see if she might catch a glimpse of Carson.

"Give me a couple of hours, okay? It takes a while to smoke brisket," she said, and Hudson jerked his attention to her in the rear-view mirror.

"Brisket?"

"Oh, that got your attention, huh?" She laughed and Hudson grinned.

"Well, yeah. I mean, brisket."

"He's a meat lover," Scarlett said.

"Most men are," Adele said. "Shoot. Should I not be making brisket? Do you think that will entice Carson?" She looked at Scarlett, who twisted from her position in the front seat. Why had she even asked that? She'd *invited* Carson to lunch. *Invited* him.

"Entice him to do what?" Scarlett asked, clear confusion in her eyes.

Adele folded her arms and said, "I don't know." She really wanted to get out of the truck, but it was still moving. Hudson pulled into Scarlett's driveway a minute later, and Adele opened the door before the vehicle stopped all the way.

She moved faster than even she knew she could, waving when she heard Scarlett call, "See you in a bit." Adele crossed the lawn and dashed up her steps and into her cabin, locking the door and pressing her back into the door behind her. Her breath came quickly, and she closed her eyes for a few moments.

"Brisket," she said, setting herself into motion. She could get the video done before she needed to cart everything across the grass to the homestead. She pulled it out of the oven and put it on the granite pieces directly under the camera.

She poked it, shredded a little bit, and determined it wasn't quite ready yet. Back in the oven, with a touch more water on the wood chips in the bottom of the roasting pan. Smoke billowed up, and she covered every-thing with aluminum foil to force it into the meat and not out of the vent at the back.

She worked through a kale salad and put a pot on her single burner to make a batch of creamed corn. She measured and pinched salt, pepper, and cornstarch, that soothing calmness she craved coming over her.

At least until someone knocked.

Adele's attention flew to the front door. She pushed her hair off her forehead, cursing this short cut she'd gotten a couple of weeks ago. Sweaty, and with too much out to hide, she stood very still.

The knocking came again, this time with Carson call-ing, "Adele?" The doorknob rattled as if he'd come in without being invited. Fury raged through her, and she was suddenly grateful that she'd bought and installed that second lock.

She practically ran across the room to the front door and said, "Lunch is at the homestead, and it's not ready yet."

"Maybe I could come in and just hang out until it is."

Adele exhaled, once again torn right in half. When he turned the knob again, she couldn't believe she'd ever found him attractive. Or that she'd been considering going out with him. That she'd invited him to this stupid lunch in the first place.

Without thinking—or maybe she'd lost her mind—she

undid the locks and pulled the door open a couple of inches. "You can't come in."

Carson stood there in those ultra-clean jeans, that cowboy hat on his head, and those gorgeous blue eyes drinking her up. "Why not?"

"You just can't."

He cocked his head and smiled, and dang if she almost didn't invite him in. "Come on."

"No," she said, stepping forward as if to block him. "I don't like people watching me cook." He was so much taller than her, and if he came closer, he'd be able to see over her head and into the kitchen.

"It smells great. I'm not going to judge you."

"Get off my porch!" she said, and it may have morphed into a yell.

Carson blinked, pure surprise flowing across his face. It was immediately replaced with a dark look, and his jaw jumped as he ground his teeth together.

"Go on," she said. "Lunch isn't ready yet."

He glared at her, and she said, "You can't come in. Have you seen anything?"

"What would I see?"

"Please just go," she said, but there wasn't any whining in her voice. More like barking.

Carson growled, moved down the steps, and said loudly, "I wasn't coming in. Jeez. I *knocked*. I didn't see anything. What are you doing in there anyway?" He shook his head as he marched away. "You know what? It doesn't matter. I don't care. You're crazy."

"You're uninvited to lunch," Adele called after him, pure fury driving her toward irrationality. Tears—actual tears—leaked down her face, and she swiped at them angrily. She couldn't believe this man had driven her to crying. She never cried.

Carson disappeared around the corner of the home-stead at the same time Scarlett moved up the steps, her face one of worry.

"Hey, sweetie." She guided Adele back toward the cabin, and she realized she'd come out on the front porch completely, leaving her cabin wide open for anyone to see.

"He is impossible," Adele said, practically a shout. "Impossible!" The yell made Scarlett flinch away from her.

Then she put her arm around Adele, who had more tears spilling down her face.

"Okay," Scarlett said. "Come on. Let's get inside." She guided Adele into her cabin, and Adele was so distraught she didn't realize what had happened until Scarlett closed the door behind them.

And now she had someone in her house. She faced Scarlett, her heart racing like it was trying to win the Kentucky Derby.

Chapter Ten

C arson showed up at the homestead the next morning, right on time. Just because he'd been uninvited to lunch and then spent the afternoon and evening alone didn't mean he wasn't going to do his job.

And Scarlett had asked to meet with him this morning.

He yawned, stifling it quickly when she called, "Come in." He couldn't let anyone know that he'd lain awake for a lot of the night. The rest of it, he'd wandered the ranch under the glow of the moon, wondering where he'd gone so wrong.

His anger and frustration with God had returned in full force, and he'd spent hours trying to figure out why he'd had to lose his ranch in Montana. Why his mother had left him alone with his dad and brother. Why, when he'd done everything right, they'd still gotten a reward and he'd been forced to leave the only life he'd ever known.

And why, when he'd been getting along so well with Adele, things had then gone so badly.

He opened the door to the homestead—which wasn't locked with double locks—and said, "Morning, Scarlett." He ducked his head and joined her at the kitchen table.

She exhaled and looked down at the various items in front of her. She had a notebook, a checkbook, several checklists, and some old papers that looked like she'd dug them out of the backyard.

"I wanted to ask you some questions," she said. "I've never run a ranch, and you have. I'd love some advice."

"I can do my best to help," he said.

"So I'd like to get the backing of this animal protection organization called Forever Friends," she started, meeting his eyes. "They're coming a week from today, and I'd like to have as many of the pieces in place to show them that Last Chance Ranch is worthy of their endorsement."

"All right."

"So I'm wondering how many people you think I need to hire." She lifted her pen and held it above the notebook, obviously ready to write.

Carson blew out his breath. "Okay, so you've got what? Five or six areas here with animals? Horses, pigs, llamas, dogs, cattle...cats." He ticked them off on his fingers. "I'd have a foreman over each one of those. That way, you've got someone to organize feeding schedules and veterinary care, who knows the animals because he or she sees them every day."

"Go on," Scarlett scribbled on her notepad.

"You've got plenty of cabins in the Community," he said. "You could get some good people." He gave her a few seconds to finish writing. "I'd hire an accountant, and I'd give all the farming and agriculture responsibilities to Sawyer as soon as you can. It'll take a full-time man to oversee crops and make sure all the dietary needs of the individual animals are met." He reached up and removed his cowboy hat to scratch the back of his head. "Maybe two men."

"Two men." She kept writing and then looked up at him. "Go on."

"I think Hudson is mapping the place already," he said. "You have so much more potential to grow the food you need. That'll cut down on costs, but you'd need more farmhands. I'd get a vet on retainer, because you have over a hundred animals here, and some of them aren't farm animals. There's a big difference between a horse and a cat. So maybe two vets—one who specializes in large animal care and one who specializes in small."

Smoke could've lifted from the tip of her pen she wrote so fast. "Forever Friends runs an adoption program," she said. "Do you think we could handle that?"

"Sure," he said. "Find the right person, and they could handle all of that." He leaned into the table. "Look, Scarlett, you own the ranch, right?"

"Right."

"So it's important for you to be seen out on the ranch,

working too. But you can't have any *main* responsibilities." He made wide, sweeping motions with both hands. "Your job is to make sure the ranch functions as a whole. If there's a problem, you want to know about it, but you don't want to fix it. You want your foreman to fix it, report to you, and tell you how it's not going to happen again. You want to be present, but not all-powerful."

Scarlett wrote and wrote, and then read over what she'd filled a couple of pages with. "I like the land wild."

"Yeah, every ranch should have a free range," he said. "But land can be wild and still be used with more potential."

"What about chickens?"

"Chickens?" he asked.

"Well, we have everything else, and it seems like the ranch needs chickens."

"Sure," he said. "Put 'em in with the pigs, and everyone'll be happy." They talked for a while longer, and she finally sat back, apparently exhausted.

"Thank you so much, Carson," she said. "This has been hugely helpful."

"Happy to do it," he said, standing and shaking her hand. "I guess I better get over to the Goat Grounds. We only have a few more days until they have to perform with people in their arena." He tipped his hat again, sure he was the picture of calm, cool, and collected as he left the homestead.

But inside, he was shaking. He didn't want to face

Adele in the Goat Grounds, the exact same way he hadn't wanted to face his father and Terry after he'd sold the ranch.

The usual disappointment tasted bitter in the back of his mouth, and his strides toward the Goat Grounds were fueled with his anger. He paused when he saw Adele in the arena with all the baby goats already. She wore a glorious smile on her face, and if anything, it only made him angrier.

How in the world could she be so happy?

She reached down and patted one of the goats, saying, "We'll have to apologize, Bubble Gum. We shouldn't have yelled at him."

Immediately, his heart softened.

She gave the little goat a piece of cracker and moved to the next one. Her voice was almost inaudible when she said, "Please, God, help me be nice to Carson."

He sucked in a breath, sure she'd hear him, but she turned further, putting her back to him, and kept moving around with the goats. She'd placed the blocks out, and she pointed with two fingers to the one she wanted the animals to jump on, treating them each time they did.

Please, God....

The thought stalled in his mind. She'd had hard things happen to her too. She hadn't told him much about her life previous to coming to Last Chance Ranch, but he'd heard some things in her voice when she'd mentioned her ex-husband. And she certainly was hiding something in that cabin.

Please, God, he thought again, trying to find a way to finish it. *Please help me be nice to her too.*

Pure peace hit him square in the chest, and it rendered him mute and still.

Be still, and know that I am God.

Carson held very still, trying to hang onto this feeling for just a few more moments. But Adele turned, caught sight of him, and looked like she might throw up.

He lifted one hand in a hesitant wave and got his feet moving toward the gate. "Hello," he said, more formality between them than he ever wanted.

She dropped her chin to her chest for a moment, then stooped to run her hand along another goat's back.

"Listen," he said. "I'm sorry about yesterday. I just... wanted to see you. Spend time with you."

She lifted her gaze to his, and something crackled between them. "I'm sorry too," she said. Nothing else. And everything seemed right back to okay between them.

"Looks like the goats have got it," he said.

"Yeah." She gave out another cracker. "So let's take a break today. Have you eaten breakfast?"

He blinked at her. "I don't eat breakfast."

"Ever?"

"I like coffee." He shrugged and looked down at one of the babies who'd wandered over to him.

"I'm asking you to take me to breakfast." Adele lifted

one eyebrow at him, and Carson flinched as he realized what an idiot he was.

"Are you asking me out?"

"No," she said with a smile. "I'm asking *you* to take *me* out." She broke the last piece of cracker she had in her hand and tossed all the crumbs into the air. "Help me get these goats back in the pasture."

"Maybe you could try asking."

"I—" Adele blinked, a beautiful blush seeping into her cheeks. "You're right. Could you help me put the goats in the pasture?"

"Sure." He clicked his tongue, and said, "Come on, guys. Time to be done." He started for the gate that led toward the barns and the pasture where the goats' parents were, and thankfully, almost all the babies came with him.

Once they had all the goats secured behind the right gate, he turned toward her, slowly—oh, so slowly—reached for her hand. Their fingers aligned, and it was like someone had sprinkled magic pixie dust on his skin and in his blood. Everything tingled, and Carson wanted to hold onto this moment for a lot longer.

"So, you haven't said much about your family," Adele said.

"You haven't either," he said.

"Okay, I'll start. I have a couple of sisters. Both younger than me. Molly is married and living back in Savannah—that's where I'm from. Wilma's been living in

Oklahoma for a decade or so now. She's been married and divorced, like me."

His fingers tightened on hers, and he said, "I'm sorry." He cleared his throat, because he had a horrible feeling he was about to tell her something he hadn't talked about with anyone. "My mom left me and my brother when I was twelve."

His throat burned, the way it had when he'd driven away from his ranch for the last time.

"Wow," she said. "My parents are divorced too. My mom's still in Georgia. Daddy went back to New Jersey."

"I don't know where my mother went."

"You don't talk to her?"

"Nope."

"And you had to sell your ranch in Montana," she said, their hands swinging between them.

"Yes," he said, wondering if it was too much to tell her everything before they'd even gotten in a car or sat at a table.

"I'm dying to know about that."

"I'm sure you are," he said, feeling a snap, crackle, and pop in his bloodstream. He drew in a big breath and then blew it out. "My dad finds his happiness at the bottom of a bottle. He has for quite a long time. So I ran the ranch for almost twenty years."

The gravel crunched under their feet for a few steps. "Scarlett seems to think you're a pretty amazing cowboy," she said.

"Well, I'm not one to brag," he said.

"So one might wonder why you had to sell the ranch you ran for almost twenty years."

"Gambling habit," he said, quickly adding, "Not mine. That would be my brother, Terry. He didn't work either—unless you count counting cards during his online poker matches." And Carson didn't count that. That didn't bring in hay or feed horses or immunize cattle.

Carson did all of that, as much as he could. He'd been right in telling Scarlett that she needed to hire people to oversee each operation at Last Chance Ranch. Carson wished he'd been able to afford that, and he sometimes wondered that if he'd gone into debt for payroll, he might've been able to keep the ranch.

How, he wasn't sure.

It was just a path his mind took from time to time.

"He gambled away any money I managed to bring in, and when the oil was discovered, I saw my opportunity to get away from both of them." Carson looked up into the clear blue sky. "Unfortunately, that meant I had to give up the ranch too."

"What was it called?" she asked.

"What was what called?"

"Your ranch."

"Oh, Cobble Creek." He could picture the snow drifts in the winter, the broad expanse of green hay in the summer. The big red barn where he kept the tractors and supplies. The twenty-horse stable, and the cowboy cabins out on the range. Sometimes he'd ride out to one and stay for as long as he dared, always having to return to the mess in the homestead.

Once, he'd come back to find Terry had gotten married over the weekend. Married. To a woman who was now living in Carson's house. He'd thought it would end quickly, but Maribel was still at Cobble Creek—and Carson wasn't.

"I can hear how much you love it," Adele said, her fingers gripping his. She reached over with her other hand and put it on his forearm.

He glanced at her to find a sweet smile on her face, one of the softest looks he'd seen. "I did love it."

"How do you like it here?"

"I'm adjusting," he said. "The weather is certainly better, but I didn't mind the snow."

"I've never lived anywhere with snow."

"That feels impossible to me," he said.

"Well, it doesn't snow much in the South," she said. "And then I came to California for college. Been here ever since."

"In the city, though, right?"

"Yeah." She sighed. "I do miss the city sometimes."

"Well, let's get you down to a more civilized area," he said, increasing his pace and hoping that maybe he'd be able to find out why she kept her cabin locked so tight.

Chapter Eleven

G et over your phobia of rich men.

Scarlett's words drifted through her head.
Over and over they echoed. Her hand felt cold without
Carson's in it, but that made no sense. It was almost July in
California, and Adele didn't normally get a chill anyway.

She fiddled with her phone while Carson got the air
conditioning blowing in his fancy truck. "This is nice," she
said, reaching out to touch the dashboard in front of her.

"I bought it when I sold the ranch," he said. "Believe
me, it's the nicest thing I've ever owned."

She looked at the expansive space between them on
the bench seat, wishing she'd been brave enough to slide
over and sit next to him. Her heart bobbed up near the
back of her throat for some reason, and she finally
narrowed it down to the fact that she was thinking about
kissing him.

Not today, she told herself. That would be way too fast, considering they'd had a screaming match on the back lawn of the homestead just yesterday. But the idea existed, and Adele cleared her throat and adjusted her straw hat on her head.

"Where do you want to go to eat?" he asked.

"I don't care," she said. She probably wouldn't be able to put anything in her mouth anyway. First dates had always made her nervous, and this one felt particularly important. The first first date after her relationship with Hank had ended.

"I have a confession," she said.

"I can't wait to hear it."

"You're my first date since my divorce."

"Is that what this is? A date?'

"It better be," she said. "So get out your wallet, Mister Moneybags."

He chuckled and shook his head. "Mister Moneybags. Good one."

"You do have a lot of money, right?"

"I have enough," he said, his voice definitely on the hedging side.

"I read about you online," she said, apparently another confession spilling from her lips.

He looked at her as they went past the robot that marked the entrance of Last Chance Ranch. He didn't really need to look at the road, because there was never anyone else on it. "You did what?"

"I looked you up," she said. "You have the *cleanest* jeans of any cowboy I've ever met."

Carson looked out the windshield, and the weight of his blue-eyed gaze gone from her face. "I don't even know what to say," he said. "My jeans?"

"How many pairs do you own?" she asked.

"Of jeans?"

"Yeah." Adele felt a flicker of flirty-ness move through her, and she seized onto it. "I mean, they are abnormally clean."

He glanced down at his legs. "I don't think they are."

"How many times do you wear them before you wash them?"

"One?" he asked, and the way he made it into a question was absolutely adorable.

"And you still haven't answered my question."

"I think I have five or six pairs of jeans." He cut her a look out of the corner of his eye. "Happy now?"

"No." She unbuckled her seat belt and slid across the seat, only slightly embarrassed when her bare backs of her legs stuck to his leather seats and made a squeaking sound. She snuggled right up next to him and wrapped his hand inside both of hers.

"Now I'm happy."

THE NEXT SEVERAL days passed in a blur of sleeping, shopping, cooking, filming, video editing, and goat training. Adele went to bed exhausted and woke up in the morning slightly less tired.

She'd toyed with the idea of taking a break from Tasty-Spot, just for a few days. Just until she knew how these goat yoga classes were going to go. But then, on Wednesday, a celebrity chef commented on one of her videos.

Best idea for leftover brisket I've ever seen.

That comment stuck in her head the same way Scarlett's words about giving Carson a chance did.

She'd responded to Joey Dawson's comment, and they'd been having a dialog for the past few days. She felt like she'd entered the Bermuda Triangle or the Twilight Zone. After all, she was just some lowly chef wannabe on a ranch in California.

Joey Dawson owned three restaurants in New York City. New. York. City.

Adele checked her phone before she got out of bed on Saturday morning. The morning light was flat and gray, because the sun hadn't risen yet. Joey hadn't commented back to her last response either, and she sighed as she swung her legs over the side of the bed and got up.

She stretched, bending down and reaching for her toes, wondering when she'd touched them last. She arched her back and twisted sideways, working the kinks out of her muscles and joints. She'd fallen asleep last night with yoga instruction videos playing on her computer.

You're ready for this, she thought, immediately followed with a quick prayer of *Please help me control the crowd this morning. Not just control them. Inspire them. Entertain them.*

She really wanted goat yoga to be a success, and not just for her. But for Scarlett too. Scarlett, who'd given her a free place to live and pretty much free reign to do whatever she wanted here as long as the cats got fed and the goat arena was in tip-top shape.

She dressed in a black pair of spandex pants, a tank top that revealed the fact that her upper arms weren't nearly as toned as they should be, and a sturdy pair of running shoes. The teal and pink stripes on her shoes matched the blue of her tank top, and she pulled her short hair into a ponytail with a pink rubber band.

When she looked at herself in the mirror, she looked like she could conduct a yoga class. She did have a certification from her time at the spa. Of course, wall yoga was completely different than goat yoga. No straw in the spa. No droppings on the floor.

But a lot less pretentious people too. She hoped.

She pulled the ponytail out, because it looked ridiculous, and her hair was already falling out. She sighed as she pinned her hair back and put on a pink visor. Carson had said he didn't eat breakfast, but food was Adele's go-to for when she was anxious or upset, happy or joyous. She didn't want to eat a ton before her class, but she did pull out one of the egg muffins she'd made a couple of weeks ago.

Thirty seconds in the microwave, and her frozen breakfast was hot and ready to eat. She followed the sausage, pepper, and egg muffin with a half a cup of coffee that had more cream and sugar than actual caffeine.

Then she left her cabin, locked the door behind her, and started toward the Goat Grounds as the sun started to lighten the day into various shades of gold.

In the arena, she used the pitchfork to spread out the half a bale of straw she'd set by the gate for this morning. She wanted there to be enough straw to cover the dirt, and she liked the way her muscles tensed and released as she worked.

Carson had said he liked to work with wood, and she'd asked him to build a bin or a chest for the yoga mats. They'd discussed putting it beside the gate, so people could take them as they checked-in.

He hadn't arrived in the Goat Grounds yet, and anxiety pulled through her. She looked over the fence and down the road, hoping to see him. He wasn't coming, and she took the pitchfork with her toward the barn. The goats wouldn't be brought out until just before the class, and she would do that.

She'd mingle with the class members, and Carson would check them in. He didn't have a printer or a computer, as he'd admitted to not really being into the digital age during their lunch at the pizza buffet on Monday.

Or maybe that had been during the picnic they'd taken on Thursday afternoon. He'd driven down to town and bought sandwiches and chips at the deli, and they'd escaped to a remote part of the ranch to eat.

And lie on their backs on the blanket he'd brought, talking and watching the sky. In Montana, he said there'd be clouds, but the California sky didn't have any of those. At least not that day.

Before she'd gone through the gate, she heard the rumble of an engine, and she spun back. Guests hadn't arrived yet, had they?

No, it was Carson's white truck that pulled into the parking lot, and he backed in to the closest space to the gate. The engine turned off, and he got out and moved around to the tailgate.

Adele's hand drifted up and pressed against her pulse, which was now firing against her breastbone. He was the picture of male perfection, from that hat to those boots and everything in between.

By the end of their lunch, he'd been laughing about the cleanliness of his jeans, and he'd promised to wear a dirty pair to goat yoga. After all, she'd told him that every cowboy should look like they belonged on the ranch where they worked.

He whistled as he reached for the huge case in the back of his truck. The bin for the mats. Adele left the pitchfork by the gate leading toward the barn, and she hurried back across the arena to him.

"Carson," she said as he reached the gate. "Let me get it. Let me. Hold on. Back up a bit."

He did, and she opened the gate and guided him through it. "Right there. Set it down there."

He once again did as she asked, and she remembered his sharp look as he'd suggested she ask him to help her. He didn't seem to mind today, though, and he stood back and smiled at the bin he'd made.

"What do you think?"

"What do I think?" Adele backed up a few steps and slipped her hand into his. "I think it's beautiful, Carson. Is that a—?" She leaned forward to examine the figure carved into the wood on the top rung of the bin.

"It's a goat," he said.

"And it says Last Chance Ranch." She turned and beamed at him. "You made this?"

"I told you I liked to work with wood."

"Yeah, but you carved something into it."

"Yeah, it's called whittling." He grinned at her and drew her into his arms. "Good morning, by the way."

"Oh, the jury's still out on that," she said, though she did enjoy the safety of his arms, the scent of his cologne. "We can decide if the morning is good *after* the class."

"Right," he said. "Only an hour now. What time did you get here?" He released her and started toward the opposite corner where the yoga mats had been stacked.

She followed him and said, "I've only been here for about twenty minutes."

"Right," he said. "I don't believe that. Did you sleep last night?"

"A little," she said, but she didn't want to tell him that some of her insomnia was because of the chicken cheese bread she'd made, filmed, and edited so she could have a video for today and one for tomorrow.

She didn't think she'd want to cook and film today, so she'd had to get ahead.

"You?" she asked.

"Oh, yeah," he said. "Slept like a baby." He picked up an armful of rolled yoga mats. "Did you know people who sleep with a dog in their bed get better rest than those who don't?"

Adele had no idea how to respond to that. She grabbed as many yoga mats as she could carry. "I did not know that."

"It's true," he said. "I heard it on the radio last night while I was finishing the case."

She could just picture him on his front porch, carving —oops, whittling—and listening to the radio, his two black labs at his feet. It was the picture of serenity and peace, and she held onto those feelings for as long as she could.

By the time they had all the mats loaded in the case, Adele's nerves had returned. She stood back and snapped a couple of pictures with her phone. "We can put these on the website."

"I'll be sure to get a lot of pictures this morning too," he said.

"And you've got the list for check-in?"

"Yep, Scarlett let me use the printer at the homestead."

"Perfect," Adele said. "And I'll work on the electronic check-in. I bet Scarlett would let us use the money we earn for an iPad or something."

"I'll need to be tutored in how to use that," he said.

"Oh, I can tutor you, cowboy," Adele said, grinning at him.

His eyes blazed with desire. "I'd like that."

Adele had always felt the fire between them. She knew he'd burn her, and yet she wanted to play with him anyway. "Goats first," she said, clearing her throat and taking a step away from him. "Class. Then tutoring."

And by "tutoring," she hoped Carson knew she meant, "kissing."

"Let's go get the goats then," he said.

"Yes," she said. "Let's go get the goats."

Chapter Twelve

C arson moved through the people down on the yoga mats, most of them with high ponytails and giggles in the backs of their throats every time a goat got close. Adele didn't miss a beat in her yoga instruction, and it took a great deal of Carson's concentration to keep the goats moving, treat them when they did what he wanted, instead of simply staring at her.

Everyone had been on time, twittering and taking pictures as they walked up. One woman had filmed the whole thing, including him checking her in. He'd given her a huge smile while internally, he was rolling his eyes. Who cared about that video?

Of course, Carson didn't really understand social media at all. The people he wanted to see and talk to, he... well, saw and talked to them in person. Sure, he texted, but posting on Facebook or something like that?

Wasn't in his wheelhouse. He wouldn't even know who would read his posts.

He treated Peanut Butter Cup as the goat jumped up and balanced on a woman in a pink shirt. Her friend on the mat beside her dropped out of her yoga pose and snapped some pictures. Carson turned to move down another alleyway between the mats, and Peanut Butter came with him, obviously not satisfied with the bit of graham cracker he'd gotten.

Carson's job was to keep the goats moving. Make sure they got to every person.

Adele finished her workout and started clapping, everyone else joining in. "And now we'll have a few minutes for pictures," she said. "Or questions. Carson and I will be available to help with either."

Carson fed the last of the crackers to the nearby goats before he was swamped with people, most holding cell phones.

Then the pyramids began. The goat-holding. The laughing and smiling and clicking of pictures. He tapped on two dozen phones, smiling and chuckling with the people. Adele worked the crowd opposite him, and Carson kept trying to catch her eye.

She either didn't want to look at him or was really involved in her conversations. Either way, their eyes never met, and by the time the last group of people left, Carson was ready for a tall glass of ice cold water.

He opened the gate for Adele to herd the goats back to

the pasture, and he grabbed the shovel and started cleaning up the arena. Adele returned with a half a bale of straw, and Carson forked it out in preparation for their next class.

It wasn't set to start until eight o'clock that night, but now they were ready.

"Wow," he said once he'd finished. "Tell me what you think."

She looked at him, rivers of excitement running through her gaze. "I think that was the most amazing thing in the world." She giggled and shrieked just before launching herself into his arms.

Carson laughed with her as they spun around. He set her on her feet again, and Adele fell back a few steps, tucking the errant pieces of her hair behind her ears. "Okay, so I'm starving," she said.

"I'm thirsty," he said. "Have you got water in your cabin?"

Adele rolled her eyes. "No, cowboy. But you have some in yours." She started for the fence and pointed him through it.

"Oh, so you can come in my house, but I can't come in yours?"

"I want to see your dogs."

"Excuses," he teased, capturing her hand in his when they hit the road.

"I...." Adele looked to her right, away from him. "I'm not ready to tell you yet."

"Tell me what?"

"Can you understand that?" she asked, serious now.

Carson wanted to give her the space and respect she wanted and deserved. So he said, "Of course I don't understand it. But you'll tell me when you're ready."

She didn't confirm, and that made Carson's stomach writhe as if he'd swallowed a handful of tiny snakes. "Right?" he pushed.

"Right," she said.

They continued to his house, where he got tall glasses of water for both of them, draining his in only a few seconds. "Wow, goat yoga is thirsty work." He filled his glass again and watched Adele sit on his couch, both Tony and Ted at her feet.

Traitors.

He shook his head as he smiled at the three of them. "Do you have pets?" he asked.

"Not right now," she said. "I did have a little dog back in the city." She scrubbed behind his big dog's ears and spoke without taking her eyes off the black labs. "But she got old, and we had to put her down."

"Oh, that's too bad."

"She drove Hank crazy," she said.

Carson breathed in and out, and then said, "Hank must be the ex-husband."

Adele froze, and Tony pushed his head under her hand to get her to keep petting him. She stood and looked at Carson instead. "Yeah," she said, drawing the word out. "He's the ex-husband."

"Where is he now?"

"I don't know."

"How long has it been?"

"Just over a year now." She smoothed her hands over her hair. "I mean, it was over long before that, but the divorce has been final for a year."

Carson nodded and turned to open the fridge. "How do you feel about omelets?"

"I adore omelets." She came up behind him. "I can make one for us, if you want."

He straightened, realizing just how close to him she stood. He lazily curled one hand around her waist and brought her close. The desire to kiss her dove through him, and his head dipped down.

"So I like ham in my omelets," she said, her voice higher pitched than Carson had heard it before. "And cheese. And sometimes broccoli. What have you got in your fridge?" Adele wiggled out of his grip, and Carson let her go.

She had a distinct edge of heat in her eyes too, but her sudden babbling and quick escape indicated she wasn't ready for him to kiss her.

Yet, he told himself.

And that was okay. He had a feeling that when he kissed Adele Woodruff, his whole life would change, and he'd just gone through a major life adjustment as it was.

"I think I have some tomatoes," he said. "What about those for an omelet?"

THE DAYS PASSED QUICKLY, with animal feedings and stall cleanings and almost more goat yoga than he could stomach. Adele always came to his house in the evenings after their sessions, and she seemed more exhausted than she should be.

Her schedule was much more open than his, as all she needed to do was feed the cats and work the yoga sessions. She did spend time in the Goat Grounds with all the goats in addition to that, but she didn't need to get up at the crack of dawn to do it.

She definitely had something going on behind that double-locked door of her cabin, but Carson refused to ask again. She'd said she'd tell him when she was ready, and Carson decided he could be patient.

After all, he'd lived with his father and brother for years as they drove the ranch further and further into debt.

"Picnic tomorrow," Adele said with a sigh as she got to her feet. She dusted off her jeans and looked down at him. They'd been sitting on his front steps while the stars came out, his hands busy with a piece of wood, both dogs beside her, and her telling him stories of her childhood in Savannah.

Carson could listen to Adele talk for hours, but she was really good at asking him questions too.

"Yeah," he said. "I'm helping with the tent and tables in the morning." He stilled his carving knife. "You're cooking everything?"

"Well, not everything. Scarlett's bringing watermelon."

"You still haven't told me how you're going to elevate a hamburger or a hot dog." She'd told him that Scarlett had asked her to do the menu, and she wanted to stay true to a traditional holiday picnic, but "elevate" it.

When he'd asked her how she was going to do that, she'd craftily dodged the question.

"Chili," she said.

"Chili," he repeated.

"Homemade chili. My grandmother's recipe." She grinned at him and extended her hand toward him. "Come on, cowboy. Walk me back to my cabin."

Carson set his carving aside and stood up. "All right." Sometimes he walked her home, and sometimes he didn't. Sometimes she drove over to his place, and sometimes he drove her back. She hadn't even gotten close to kissing him, and Carson had decided to let her make the first move.

"Jeri's bringing a salad."

"Mm," Carson said. "The ranch really has grown in the last couple of weeks."

"Well, Scarlett has money coming in now," she said.

"Hudson sold all those cars. The goat yoga is on fire. And Forever Friends has provided a huge grant."

"Yeah." Carson knew what was going on around the ranch. It felt like a miniature community up here, the same way Cobble Creek had been. Scarlett had hired someone to oversee the cattle, and Cache Bryant had taken the cabin on the other side of Hudson. Carson had moved in next to Sawyer, and Jeri Bell had taken the one next to him.

Another new hire, a general handyman and fix-it man, David Merrill, rounded out the inhabitants in the Community.

Carson liked them all, though he saw some more than others. Jeri was working on the new canine construction, but apparently she could spare some time to put together a salad.

Adele didn't say much else on the way back to her cabin, and Carson followed her lead. He paused at the bottom of her steps, knowing better than to go up them. "Adele?" he asked, something low and serious in his voice.

She must've heard it, because she turned back and just looked at him.

"You believe in God, right?"

"Yes, sir," she said simply.

He gazed up into the night sky, the vastness of it almost suffocating him. The stars winking back at him used to be a testament of the Lord's all-powerful and all-knowing presence in Carson's life.

"At times like these, I think I do too."

Adele came back down the steps and moved right into Carson's arms. "What happened?" she asked.

"I begged Him to let me keep the ranch," Carson said, his eyes drifting closed as his voice dropped to a whisper. "And that didn't happen. I lost it. I lost it all."

Adele held onto him, and Carson was glad for the tight grip of her arms around his back. It felt like she was holding him together in a crucial moment. "Have you ever wondered if maybe He thought you shouldn't be there anymore?"

Instant anger flared inside him, cooling almost as fast as it had come. "I guess."

"Just think about it," she said, taking a step back and letting her hands linger on his arms. "If you still had the ranch in Montana, you wouldn't be here. We wouldn't have met."

And with that, she turned and went up the steps, unlocked her door, and disappeared inside.

Carson didn't want to go back to his empty cabin, so he whistled for the dogs, and together, the three of them set off down the road. He craved the silence, the glow of the moon on the gravel in front of him, and the clarity of mind to truly consider what Adele had said.

Step by step, Carson realized that he too believed in God. He always had. He'd just lost his way for a while—was still wandering in strange paths.

"Help me," he whispered into the night, feeling the

spark of life coming back into him. Something hot burned in his chest where his heart had just been a lump for so long.

"I'm sorry," he said next. "Help me find where I'm supposed to be."

And for the first time in his almost forty years of life, Carson could envision a life of happiness somewhere other than Cobble Creek Ranch.

Chapter Thirteen

Adele chopped onions while the ground beef browned. The camera recorded above her, and step by step, ingredient by ingredient, she made the pot of chili and transferred it to a Crock pot to stay warm.

There wasn't anything terribly special about a chili cheese dog—except that it fit her theme for the week of upscale and yet down-home traditional favorites for outdoor dining.

Yes, it had taken her an hour to come up with the right combination of words for the theme, but it was work she enjoyed. Good thing too, because her exhaustion was reaching peak levels, and she felt a crash coming.

She sliced tomatoes for the hamburgers, and started a skillet to caramelize the onions. She mashed ripe avocados with cilantro, onion, and more tomato to make a home-made guacamole. If there was something better than caramelized onions and guac on a hamburger, Adele wasn't sure she wanted to know.

She'd probably gain twenty pounds if she knew of such a food.

She tore lettuce, cut the homemade hamburger buns she'd made the day before, and got condiments out of the fridge.

With everything set, she took a rare moment to just sit and look at her phone. She hadn't been able to interact as much with her TastySpot viewers in the past few weeks as she had initially. Number one, the goat yoga was tiring physically. Number two, any free time she had, she wanted to spend with Carson.

But she opened the app now and started going through her videos. "What in the world?" she said aloud when she saw that her video from last Friday on the hidden cheeseburger had received four times as many views, likes, and comments as usual.

Her eyes flew to the top of the screen, where her followers were listed.

"Doubled." She leaned closer, as if her old eyes hadn't seen correctly. "Almost triple. What happened?"

She didn't have the time or energy to comb through two hundred comments to find out what had happened. Her views were up to two hundred thousand on that video, and she couldn't fathom why.

It wasn't like hers was the only video to show how to press a cube of cheese into the center of seasoned ground beef. Sure, she'd made a three-cheese pimento, but that wasn't special. Was it?

Apparently it was.

The pressure behind her eyes increased, and pure panic raced through her. What if her videos weren't good enough after this? What if her recipes became pedestrian? What if she ran out of ideas?

She hadn't heard from Joey Dawson for a while, but she wasn't surprised. The man was a celebrity chef in New York City. He didn't care about her ranch food—if she could even call it that.

Sighing, she got up off the couch and went to the front door. It was time to get this show on the road. Or rather, this food on the table. She opened her front door and poked her head out just enough to see what was happening in the back yard.

The tent had been set up, and several people worked underneath it to get tables and chairs in place. She caught Scarlett's eye, who immediately dropped the napkins she was holding and came toward her.

Adele ducked back inside as Scarlett closed the last few feet and went up the steps. "Hurry," she hissed from inside the house.

"Why?" Scarlett said, entering the cabin a moment later. Adele quickly closed the door and locked it.

"Did you make guacamole?" Scarlett practically ran into the kitchen, where the bowl of guacamole sat. "You did. Adele." She gazed lovingly at the condiment and then smiled at her friend. "Guacamole is my love language."

"I know, sweetie." She reached over and tucked Scarlett's hair behind her ear. "How are things going with Hudson?" Why had she asked that? She gave herself a mental shake. If she went around asking Scarlett questions like that, they'd get tossed back at her, and she'd have to confess her soft feelings for Carson.

"You gestured me wildly over here to ask about my boyfriend?" Scarlett's eyebrows stretched toward her hairline.

"No, I wanted you to taste the chili and make sure it's not too hot." Adele opened a drawer and took out a spoon. "Wait, wait, wait." She adjusted the lighting on the bowl and pressed the button on the video camera. "All right, you'll get to be in one of the videos."

"Oh, so I'm a hand model now." Scarlett looked like a kid in a candy store, and she moved toward the bowl.

"Wait, wait," Adele said.

"What?" she asked.

"You have to do it slowly. Slower than you think you need to. And then you're going to do the same thing with a fork and the hot dog." She pointed to the ready and waiting chili dog, which looked beautiful under the bright lights.

"Okay, slowly," Scarlett confirmed. She moved her spoon through the chili slowly and tasted it. Scarlett always had possessed the best poker face on the planet, and Adele couldn't even tell if she liked it.

"Too hot?"

"It's the best chili in the world," Scarlett said. "And it's not too hot at all."

Satisfaction and pride flowed through Adele. Enough to make her smile. "Okay, hot dog." She moved it closer and nudged a bowl of cheese too. "It's a chili cheese dog. Okay, go."

Scarlett sprinkled cheese on the hot dog—slowly—and then cut off a bite with a fork. The camera wouldn't capture her eating it, but Adele watched with rapt attention anyway. She wanted people to like her food, and she was prepared to skip the barbecue completely if the food was deemed disgusting.

"Mm, Adele, you're a goddess."

Scarlett couldn't know how much her compliments meant to Adele. She felt like someone had put light bulbs in her veins and had just flipped the switch. She needed to figure out how to get to culinary school sooner rather than later, but she didn't have time to think about it right now. She'd need a notebook, and plans, ideas, and thoughts to come together before she could do anything.

"Okay, help me get all this stuff outside," she said. "And don't let anyone in." She picked up the Crock pot full of chili and nodded toward the bag of cheese and a bag of hot dog buns. "We'll have to make a couple of trips to get the caramelized onions and other toppings for the burgers."

Scarlett did what Adele asked, making three trips to get all the condiments out to the serving table. With the Muenster cheese, caramelized onions, and guacamole on the table, Adele laid the slices of tomato on the grill. They'd be there for literally twenty seconds, just to get the smoky flavor and a bit of char.

She wished she had the ability to film outside, and a whole new idea bloomed inside her mind. She did live on a ranch... And her themes were about rustic, down-home cooking. Why shouldn't she be grilling?

You could grill indoors, she thought, a whole new theme week entering her mind, seemingly completely formed and planned. Her fingers twitched to have a pen and paper, but she settled by pulling out her phone and thumb-tapping in a few notes to herself.

Jeri arrived, and she was a bosomy brunette that had a quick wit and loads of personality.

"Heya," Jeri said, carrying a huge white bowl, as she arrived. "Potato salad." She had long, dark hair, tons of jokes and puns and quips hiding just beneath her surface, and a quick smile. Adele liked her, and she'd half-hoped Jeri would take the empty cabin next to hers and Gramps.

But she hadn't, and she lived over in the Community with Carson and the other cowboys.

"You're kidding," Scarlett said, taking the bowl from the construction foreman.

"No." Jeri looked from Scarlett to Adele and back. "She said I could make any side salad I wanted, and my mom has a killer potato salad recipe."

"No, no, it's fine," Scarlett said. "It's just my favorite." She grinned at Jeri. "And Adele made guacamole, which is also my favorite. I think you guys are trying to get me to gain weight." She laughed, and Adele joined in.

"Mm, then there would be more of you to love," Hudson said from behind her, snaking one hand around her waist.

"Oh, geez," Adele said under her breath, but Scarlett giggled as she turned into Hudson.

"Yeah, you know how I feel about that." She grinned up at him, obviously smitten. This was why Adele didn't want anyone to know about her and Carson. They spent most of their time with the goats—which was work—or in his house. Last night, they had sat on the porch, but they hadn't seen anyone.

Adele focused on adjusting the heat on the grill while Scarlett stepped back. "Adele is making hamburgers to order, since there's only a few of us."

"You think eleven is a few?" Hudson asked.

"Few enough to make hamburgers to whatever temperature people want," Adele said, opening the lid on the grill. "So we're ready to start," she said to Scarlett. Then she opened a package of hot dog buns and laid them onto the hot grill rack. Just a little toasty. Get them warm, smoky, and crisp.

Then she faced the tables that had been set up as Scarlett said to Hudson, "You wanna whistle and get everyone over here?" The volunteers had set up a badminton net and a set of horseshoes in the shade along the side of the house, and they were playing over there.

Hudson puckered his lips and an ear-splitting whistle rent the air.

"Time to get started," Scarlett called, and everyone came over, including Carson. He positioned himself right next to Adele, who suddenly felt like the heat from the sun and the grill and Caron's nearness was way too much for her system.

Her knees gave a little, but she managed to stay upright—especially when Carson brushed his fingers against hers and then pulled away.

She turned back to the grill after Scarlett's speech, welcoming everyone to Last Chance Ranch, and put down a few hamburger patties. Getting everyone the protein they wanted at the requested temperature took quite a few minutes, which was just fine with Adele.

She didn't want to sit by Carson for some reason. Didn't want to make a big deal about their blooming relationship. She wanted to hold it close, tight inside her fist, the same way she did her cooking videos and social media accounts.

By the time she made her own gourmet burger and sat next to Jeri, almost everyone had finished eating. "Thanks,

Adele," Jeri said with a grin. "I'm going to go play badminton."

"Mm," Adele said around a mouthful of beef and onions. "Adele?"

She turned toward Sawyer, who'd been working on the ranch when she and Scarlett had shown up. "Hey, Sawyer." She noticed that he'd only eaten half of his chili cheese dog. "Is the chili too spicy?"

"No, it's great," he said, pushing his plate away. "Listen, I was wondering if you'd like to get lunch one day."

Adele blinked, so taken by surprise she didn't know what to say. She glanced around for Carson, sure he'd swoop in and claim her as his. They hadn't exactly hidden the hand-holding after their yoga sessions. Had they?

Adele didn't see Sawyer a whole lot, so it was possible that he didn't know about the little relationship that had started between her and Carson.

"Hey," Scarlett said, sitting down. "What's going on? Lunch was so great, Adele."

"Thanks," she said, her vocal cords working just fine now. She flicked a glance toward Sawyer, completely unsure what to do or say.

"I just asked Adele out," Sawyer said, his lips quirking up into a half-smile.

"Oh." Scarlett looked back and forth between them. Her eyes practically glowed from within. "And what did Adele say?"

"She didn't answer," Sawyer said.

Scarlett nudged Adele, and Adele wished her eyes had laser capabilities. She'd give almost anything to have mind reading powers, so she could let Scarlett know how she felt about Carson, and what had really been going on at the Goat Grounds all these weeks.

"She works so hard with the goats," Scarlett said. "Hardly ever gets off the ranch. I'm sure she'd *love* to go to lunch sometime."

"So what do you say, Adele?" Sawyer asked, and she had the distinct impression that he and Scarlett had set this whole thing up. How could her best friend do this to her? Couldn't she tell that Adele had eyes for Carson?

Scarlett kicked her under the table, and Adele kicked her right back. "She says yes," Scarlett said. "That's an order from the ranch owner."

A sense of hopelessness filled her. Maybe she could just say yes and break the date later—before Carson found out.

She smiled as sweetly as she could though her stomach clenched against the food she'd eaten. "Yes," she said, glancing around to make sure Carson hadn't heard.

Chapter Fourteen

Carson didn't see Adele for a couple of days. They'd taken a break from the morning goat yoga for the holidays, and she'd told him she was planning to sleep for days.

She had looked extremely tired for the past couple weeks, and he didn't want to bother her. Hudson had invited him and Sawyer to come out on the mapping expeditions he'd been doing for Scarlett.

Carson figured he didn't have anything else to do, and he hadn't been horseback riding for a while. So he saddled Moonbeam and led him outside to the pasture where Sawyer was already waiting.

Hudson came out last, and the three of them set off at a slow walk. Trixie, Hudson's horse, led the way, and Carson was content to simply ride in the sunshine. The silence poured through him like warm water, and he felt the same peace and serenity he'd felt the night he'd walked Adele home under all those stars.

He still hadn't gone to church, but he'd been talking to God a lot more, and he didn't feel the same anger punching through him that he had for the past year or so.

"I'm headed off the ranch for a few days this weekend," Hudson said, breaking the quiet of the wild ranch. "Can you two cover my responsibilities with the horses and llamas?"

"Off the ranch?" Sawyer asked. "Where you goin'?"

"Just to the beach," Hudson said. "The ocean clears my head."

"I'm sure we can cover it," Carson said, because Hudson did whatever Scarlett said, and while he did quite a bit of work with the horses, it wasn't so much that Carson himself couldn't do it.

"Thanks." Hudson let the silence descend again, but only for a few steps. "Scarlett's comin'," he said.

Surprise cut through Carson's previous peace. And he could admit that he was jealous. He'd been holding Adele's hand, and helping her with those goats, and driving himself crazy with thoughts of kissing her.

"So you two must be getting along great," he finally said.

"Well enough," Hudson said.

"Must be serious if you're going on a trip together."

Hudson was a man of few words—someone just like Carson and who Carson could appreciate. He said nothing now, which only drove the green-eyed monster in Carson's chest toward madness.

"He can't even confirm it," Sawyer said. "Must be *really* serious."

"It's...been about eight weeks," Hudson said. "So it's still new." He sounded wise and mature, and Carson wished he didn't feel so hormonal for the blonde woman who wouldn't even let him inside her cabin.

Not only that, she wouldn't even tell him what she was doing inside the cabin.

Hudson scanned the horizon and said, "Ho," to get Trixie to stop. He pulled out the notebook from the saddlebag behind him. "Okay, so I've got this grove here." He flipped pages until he found the section he wanted. "We stick here and go west until we get to the cemetery."

"There's a cemetery out here?" Sawyer asked.

"I think it's for the animals," he said. "The headstones are interesting. Only first names on most of them. A few say things like, 'Beloved companion to Ben.'"

"Interesting," Sawyer said. "Have you told Scarlett about it?"

"Not yet." Hudson made notes on his paper, and Carson glanced up into the sky, wishing the Lord would give him a message—a way to take things to the next level with Adele. He'd been thinking a lot about what she'd said.

If you still had the ranch in Montana, you wouldn't be here. We wouldn't have met.

She was right, and Carson *was* glad he'd met her. If

only he could tell where she stood, how she felt. She was an expert in flirting, and Carson didn't mind so much, only that she didn't seem keen on doing much more than that.

"So I asked Adele to lunch," Sawyer said, and Carson whipped his attention to the other cowboy. Something cold and hollow filled his chest, but he didn't want either of the other men to know.

"Oh, boy," Carson said, ignoring Hudson's look. "What did she do? Slam the door in your face? Roll her eyes?"

Sawyer looked at him evenly. Blinked once. "She said yes."

"What?" Carson's shock permeated his voice, his every cell, and the air. Adele had said yes to a date with Sawyer? So much was wrong with that, and he instantly knew he'd made a mistake by not kissing her when he'd had the chance.

Lots of chances, actually.

But he didn't want a broken nose, and he knew that Adele had the power to skin him alive with a single look.

Sawyer shrugged. "She actually said it would be nice to get off the ranch for a meal or two."

"I've asked her to dinner at least five times," Carson said. He looked at Hudson, his disbelief fading into fury. "What in the world is going on?"

"I don't know," Hudson said at the same time Sawyer said, "I didn't know you liked her, Carson. I'm sorry."

"I *don't* like her," Carson said darkly, trying to find the right term for how he felt about her. He did like her. Oh, he liked her a whole lot. "I only follow her around like a lovesick puppy, doing every single thing she barks at me." He continued to mutter under his breath, the other two cowboys forgotten. Their conversation continued, but Carson couldn't focus on it. All he could think about was getting back to the ranch, finding Adele, and kissing her.

The mapping expedition seemed to take hours and hours, and then he had to brush down Moonbeam and put her out to pasture. By the time he started for the cabins that lined the back yard of the homestead, he was practically running.

His boots stomped on the gravel, and Carson tried to tame his anger back into the box where it simmered, out of sight.

The cabin had a back door, and he wondered if she kept it as secure as the front. He wasn't going to open it without knocking. *You're not going to open it at all*, he told himself as he took the steps two at a time.

He pounded on the door, cringing at the negativity in the sound. "Adele," he called. If she didn't open the door, he'd call her until she answered. He'd go check the Goat Grounds. He had to find her, talk to her, figure out what the heck was going on.

Because this thing pulsing between them needed to be satisfied somehow, and if that meant a yelling match like the one they'd had in the grocery store parking lot, then he'd take it.

"Adele," he called again.

"What?" she asked, and he spun toward the sound of her voice. She stood on Gramps's back porch, her hands on her cocked hips.

He looked at her, the fight suddenly gone from his body. Now, everything just hurt. Especially his heart. "Is it true? You're going out with Sawyer Smith?"

Even from ten yards away, he saw the panic parade across her face. "You found out."

"We all live on this same piece of land," he said. "You thought you could hide it?"

"No."

He went down the steps and approached her, his fingers curled into fists. "I don't want to play games with you," he said. "I thought *we* were starting something. You go around holding hands with everyone? Cuddling up to them on their porches? Because I live next door to Sawyer, and I haven't seen you over there." He pointed as if she could see the cabins over in the Community from here.

"I don't hold hands with everyone."

"Everyone with a cowboy hat."

"No."

"Then what is going on?"

She sighed as she came down the steps, and it looked like she rolled her eyes. That made Carson's anger flare back to life.

"You know what?" he asked. "You really are crazy."

"I am not."

"Tell me you don't like me," he practically shouted as she came toward him. "And I'll leave you alone. But I like you. And I don't want you going to lunch with Sawyer-Blasted-Smith." His chest heaved, and he couldn't get enough air.

"I'm not going to go to lunch with him." Her eyes blazed with blue fire, and dang if Carson didn't want to get burned by it.

Carson opened his mouth to argue, but his brain caught up just in time. "What?"

Adele swept right into his personal space, tipped up on her toes, and kissed him.

Bright spots of light exploded behind his closed eyes, and he growled deep in his throat, grabbing onto her waist and pulling her tight against him.

"I'm not crazy," she said against his lips.

"I know," he whispered, matching up their mouths again. "I'm sorry. I didn't mean that."

She kissed him like he'd never been kissed before, and Carson felt a buzzing way down in the souls of his feet.

"I really like you," she said, her breath hot against his cheek as she tipped her head back, giving him access to the curve of her neck. Carson kissed her there, the feel of her in his arms making him light-headed.

He wanted to tell her he liked her too, but he brought his mouth back to hers and kissed her, kissed her, kissed her, hoping she'd get the message just the same.

Chapter Fifteen

Adele held Carson's face in both of her hands, the feel of his jaw, his beard, like magic against her skin. She'd been avoiding him for a few days—and catching up on some much-needed rest and relaxation.

But there was nothing to avoid about this kiss.

As soon as she'd heard that he'd gone out with Hudson and Sawyer to do some sort of mapping activity, she'd freaked out. Scarlett hadn't understood, until Adele had admitted that she and Carson were becoming more than friends.

He'd said he hadn't dated much back in Montana, but Adele didn't care. The man could kiss, and every cell in her body vibrated with the smell of him, the touch of him, the taste of him.

He finally pulled away, his breathing ragged, and his shoulders heaving slightly. "All right then," he said hoarsely. Their eyes met, and Adele didn't try to hide any of the emotions tumbling through her. "You want me to talk to Sawyer?" he asked.

"No, I can do it," she said, leaning her forehead against his collarbone. They breathed together, and Adele's gratitude for this place ran through her. *Thank you*, she prayed, not sure what she was thankful for but feeling the need to express it.

"You wanna walk with me?" she asked.

"Depends."

She slid her hands across his shoulders—wow, he had great shoulders—and down his arms to her fingers. "On what?"

"On where you're going." He bent to pick up his cowboy hat, which had fallen off at some point during their kiss.

"I thought I'd walk down to the intersection and back. It's mostly shady at this time of day."

"What's down there?"

"Nothing."

"So why are we going?"

"Just because." Adele gave him a sly smile. "I can go myself." She started to stroll, and he immediately fell into step beside her.

"I didn't mean to call you crazy," he said, his head tipped down now. He reached up with his free hand and pressed the hat to his head. "I was just so...jealous. Angry."

"I didn't really say yes," she said, and then she went on

to explain how the "date" with Sawyer had happened. "I'm not interested in him, Carson."

"I believe you," he said.

Adele breathed in deep and exhaled. "I do love it here."

"It's a nice ranch," he said. "We found a couple of old cabins out on the wild land. I always loved going out to a remote cabin when we had to gather the herd or check on crops. I loved the isolation of it. The tranquility."

Adele smiled and swung their hands between them. "So you think you'll stay here for a while?"

"Got no place else to go."

"You have a lot of money. Why don't you buy another ranch?"

Carson exhaled and adjusted his hat again. "I've thought about it. I just don't think I'm ready."

"I understand that." Adele didn't feel ready to do much of anything. And yet, she got up every day and did her best. "I came here because I was ready for a change, but I wasn't sure what that should be."

"Have you found it?"

"Sort of," she hedged. "I told you I really like cooking."

"Right. You should go to culinary school. The goat yoga is bringing in a lot of money."

Adele let several strides go by, hoping the right words would come to her mind. They didn't, and she realized she was going to have to tell him things no one but Scarlett knew. A river of fear cascaded through her, but it wasn't as strong as it once had been.

"My ex-husband skipped town," she started slowly, still trying to organize all the information. She could still feel the utter shock when she realized what Hank had done. She'd sat in her favorite window seat and watched the ocean roll in, steady and strong. She had not been steady and strong in those first few weeks. Sometimes now she didn't feel steady or strong.

"I don't know where he is. I haven't spoken to him in years. He didn't contest the divorce, nor any of the stipulations in it."

"Is that normal?" Carson asked, his hand warm against hers.

"Not really," she said. "But if he returned and faced me in court, he'd have to take responsibility for his debts." She watched the horizon, remembering how she'd wished she could disappear into it. At least she wasn't in that dark place again.

"Debts he'd made careful plans to put in my name," she said. "So the credit card companies don't care that he's the one who spent the money. What they know is my name is on the account, and they want their payment."

"No," Carson said, the word made almost entirely of air. "How much?"

"Over a hundred thousand dollars." Saying it out loud made it so much bigger. The weight of Hank's debt hovered over her, and she struggled to draw a decent breath. "So I'm making payments, and saving a little for culinary school, and if I'm lucky, I can go before I'm eighty."

"I can pay for it," he said, his voice so quiet, she thought perhaps it had been the breeze whispering through the trees.

"No," she said immediately, and loudly, just in case he had offered to pay for her culinary school. "I'm a big girl, Carson. I'm fine."

He squeezed her hand and leaned down to press his lips to her temple. "I'm sorry. That situation sounds unfair and just wrong."

"It is."

They reached the gate and kept walking. Adele cast a look toward the robot mailbox, noting how quaint and nostalgic it was. "I used to come to the ranch with Scarlett when we were in college."

"Yeah?"

"Yeah. There are a lot of good memories here."

The shade kept her mostly cool, and she was glad she'd been able to get one of her secrets out into the open. Now she just had to tell him about the cooking and the videos. She wasn't even sure why she wanted to keep it a secret. Scarlett knew, and if her trip to the beach with Hudson was any indication, he knew too.

So why couldn't Carson know?

"Can I ask you a question?" he asked, his voice serious and somewhat soothing.

"Of course."

"Why didn't you get mad at God?" he asked. "I mean, you were dealt a rotten hand. Thousands of dollars of someone else's debt? How is that fair?"

Adele heard the hurt in Carson's voice. She'd seen it in his face in previous conversations they'd had. "It's not fair," she said. "And I was upset for a while. Hank had left almost everything in the house. I sold what I could. I found out he had a storage unit, and I went and cleaned that out too."

She was treading on dangerous ground now, and she carefully veered away from telling him what she'd found in the storage locker. "I sold whatever I could from that too. Every little penny I can, I'm using to try to...." She didn't know how to finish.

"Get your life back," Carson supplied, and it fit really well.

"Yeah," she said.

"What if you can't get your life back?"

"You mean like how you'll never get Cobble Creek back?" She watched him as the muscle in his jaw started to jump.

"Yeah, like that."

"I guess—I mean—I suppose...I don't want that life back. So it sucks what happened to me. I don't deserve to be burdened with certain things. But at the same time, I made choices that got me there too."

"You did?"

"Yes," she said, her voice now barely audible. "I stayed with him when I knew his businesses were going under. I stayed when I knew he wasn't being faithful to me. I stayed, because my life was comfortable, and I was foolish, and...yeah." She shrugged, never having articulated her situation quite like that before.

"I stayed too," he finally said as they came out from under the trees that bordered the road that ran up to the ranch.

"Why did you stay?" Adele stopped walking and looked at him.

He wouldn't face her but looked west as if he might be able to see the ocean from here. "Because I knew what it felt like to have someone walk out on you. Walk away. Never look back." His eyes met hers. "And I never wanted to do that to someone."

Adele nodded, a quiet smile touching her mouth. She reached up and cradled his face in her palm. "I know what that's like too."

He dropped his chin, almost a nod of acknowledgement. Of what, she wasn't sure. It had taken Adele a solid year to come to terms with her losses. Sometimes she still wondered if this ranch life was the one she was now living, and how she'd come to be at Last Chance Ranch.

Then she'd remember that the Lord had always led her to exactly where she needed to be, exactly when she needed to be there. He'd done the same for Carson too. He just didn't know it yet.

EMERGENCY. 911.

Adele glanced at Scarlett's message on the desk beside her. She had three videos to edit, and she'd be free for a few days. She was really looking forward to it too, because Scarlett was going on a weekend getaway with Hudson, and Adele wanted to tell her about Carson while she was gone.

For some reason, she liked keeping things close to the vest in the beginning. "Probably so you can plan how to reveal them," she muttered. She couldn't help it if she was a planner. It wasn't a crime to be organized and have a game plan.

Emergency? she sent back to Scarlett.

Packing 911. Come quick.

Adele abandoned her video of the cheesy stuffed peppers—which had taken four hours of her time this week, after nightly goat yoga sessions—and typed out *On my way* as she left her cabin.

When she entered the homestead where Scarlett lived, the energy buzzed with tension.

"Scarlett?" she called.

"Swimming suit!" Scarlett yelled from the bedroom, and Adele went down the hall and paused in the door-way. It looked like a department store had been bombed.

"I can't believe I'm so nervous." Scarlett ran her hands

down her stomach, her eyes glued to her body. "The beach. I can't go to the *beach* with him."

Adele entered the room and picked up Scarlett's black suit. She tucked it into Scarlett's open suitcase. "Of course you can. You've already said yes, and you're leaving in an hour." She gave Scarlett a pointed look she hoped said *Honestly, honey. Why'd you wait so long to call?* "Which is why you should've let me come help you pack last night."

"I didn't sleep at all last night," Scarlett said, pacing from the bed to the door. "This is a bad idea, right?" She met Adele's eye, and Adele shook her head.

"Come sit for a second." She patted the bed beside the suitcase, and Scarlett came and sat next to her. "Honey, you like this man, right?"

"Yes." Scarlett sounded so miserable about it. Adele had a feeling she'd probably sound the same way about Carson. Because there was always a but. *Yes, but….*

"And he likes you," Adele prompted.

Scarlett looked down at her hands, her usually perfectly manicured nails rough from her work on the ranch. "Yes," she whispered.

"Then just let go of whatever fear is brewing inside you and go have fun."

"But the swimming suit—"

"Girl, he's seen you. He's touched your waist and arms and if he doesn't know what you've got by now, he's blind."

"I don't think he's blind," Scarlett said.

Adele laughed and shook her head. "Of course he

isn't. Scarlett, you are what you are. Your body is beautiful, and Hudson knows it."

Scarlett clenched her fingers together and then released them. "You're right."

"Of course I'm right." Adele looked at the suitcase. "Okay, pajamas. I don't think we've put those in yet." She started to get up, but Scarlett put her hand on Adele's arm.

"Why are you going out with Sawyer instead of Carson?"

"I—" Adele snapped her mouth shut, her eyes widening instead. She wanted to burst with the secret of her and Carson's kiss last week. At the same time, if she told Scarlett now, she'd never go on the beach trip with Hudson, and she needed to go.

So many thoughts ran through her mind.

This ranch.

Carson.

Culinary school.

TastySpot.

Joey Dawson.

Carson.

Her channel was making more and more money, and the tiny bit of hope she'd acquired over the past few weeks felt like a leaky balloon. She'd never get enough. She might never run out, but she'd definitely never have enough.

Her shoulders slumped and she finally said, "He's not in the plan, you know? You're the one who runs off and does things willy-nilly. I'm the planner, remember?" She

studied Scarlett, wishing she could make her friend understand. But Scarlett had always been the leaper while
Adele stood on the dock and looked.

"You can't plan your whole life," Scarlett said.

"Yes, I can." Adele stood up, this conversation now
over. "Now, do you want something a little sexier for pajamas, or are we going with the middle-aged woman look?"

"I'm too old to try for sexy," Scarlett said, causing
Adele to scoff and wave her hand.

"Rubbish. You're never too old for sexy." She stepped
over to Scarlett's dresser and opened the top drawer. A
pair of silky, purple pj's sat there. "Oh, these will do nice-
ly." She turned, grinned, and put the pajamas in Scarlett's
suitcase. Another item off her checklist. Another plan
completed.

As she walked back to her cabin, she decided she just
needed to make a new plan. A new list.

One that included culinary school *and* Carson
Chatworth.

Chapter Sixteen

Carson held the reins of the huge black horse while Cache Bryant, a cattle rancher from Nevada who Scarlett had hired to deal with the herd already here on the ranch, muttered under his breath from the rear of the horse.

Most of the animals at Last Chance Ranch had some sort of special need, whether that was a health problem or a neglect issue. This particular horse—Cowboy—walked with a limp from a previous injury, and that meant he did not like anyone poking at his hooves.

Which was too bad, because Cache and Carson wanted Cowboy to have the best life possible. And that meant re-shoeing him to make sure he could walk as well as possible.

"Almost got it," Cache called.

Cowboy tried to move, and Carson shushed him and

held the reins tight. "Just a few more minutes," he said to the horse. He never tried to soothe a horse who was just being stubborn. Cowboy could learn to stand there and get his feet taken care of.

Sure enough, a few minutes later, Cache declared the shoe done, and Carson kept a grip on the reins until the other cowboy moved out from behind the horse. Cowboy huffed and wandered away as if he didn't have a care in the world.

Cache chuckled at him and clapped the dust from his hands. "That horse."

"He's a character," Carson said, moving down the fence where they'd tied all the horses. It was inspection day, and then he had work to do in LlamaLand for Hudson, who'd taken Scarlett to the beach.

He checked the next horse while Cache held the reins, but Hero still had good shoes. He also had long scars down his right flank, and Carson lovingly traced his fingers along them as he moved toward the horse's head. "All right, boy," he said. "You're good to go." He unbridled the horse and let him walk away to a greener patch of grass.

"So what brings you to Last Chance Ranch?" he asked Cache. Carson had loved the sense of family on his ranch in Montana, and since they had a baker's dozen of cabins over in the U-shaped Community, he wanted to feel that sense of belonging again.

Cache had come to the ranch a day or two before the

Fourth of July picnic, and he'd been assessing the needs of the cattle and getting his own dairy cows situated since.

"You really want to know?" he asked.

"Yeah," Carson said as they switched places for the next horse.

Cache checked the front feet while Carson unlooped the reins from the fence. "Why do I always get the ones who need work?" He flashed a quick smile at Carson and reached into his tool belt for a chisel. "Lady Godiva, where have you been, huh?" He started working on the mare's hoof. "So I grew up on a dairy farm in Nevada. My dad was the meanest old man you ever knew."

Carson seriously doubted that, because Cache's smile was so quick. He went to church with the others too. And he didn't carry an ounce of darkness in him. So his dad didn't drink himself to sleep every night, after a rage about how poorly Carson had been running the ranch.

He expected the flood of familiar bitterness to overtake him, drown out Cache's words. But surprisingly, it only lifted through him a fraction of what it used to. And it receded quickly too, so Carson only missed a bit of Cache's story.

"Anyway, the Bureau came in, and we went to court over grazing rights." He shook his head, his face turning hard for a breath as he moved around to Lady Godiva's other side. "Years we spent in court. We stayed on the land that whole time, despite the BLM's threats to kick us off."

He lifted her leg, deemed that hoof okay, and moved to the back leg.

"We had to leave when the courts ruled in favor of the government. My dad had been farming that land for fifty years."

"How'd he get it if it wasn't his?" Carson asked.

"He bought it from an old guy. Turned out the guy worked for the BLM and should've never sold the land." Cache came back around the front of Lady Godiva. "Those back hooves look great. You're good to go, Lady." He unlatched her bridle and she lumbered away.

"So I loaded up all the cows I could and brought them here. It's been a real blessing."

A real blessing. The words reverberated through Carson's head. He smiled at Cache, and they moved to the next horse. "Surely you had more than a hundred head," he said.

"Yeah, my brother took the rest to his buddy's place in the Texas panhandle. Shiloh Ridge. I thought sunshine sounded better than snow." He chuckled. "So here we are."

"And your parents?"

"Mama died a few years back." Cache quieted for a minute, and Carson worked on Reddington's front hooves, both of which needed to be re-shod. He filed and shaped and nailed before Cache spoke again.

"Dad went with Leo to Shiloh Ridge. It's a bigger operation, already running cattle and with all the milking equipment. They took about five hundred cows with them."

"So you had a decent sized operation."

"Oh, yeah. We were doing great." Cache sounded the teeniest bit wistful.

Carson finished the shoes in the front and moved to the Reddington's back feet. He was grateful he didn't have to look at Cache when he asked, "What about you? Where'd you come from?"

Carson flinched, but the lump that usually blocked his throat from telling the tale of how he'd lost Cobble Creek didn't form. So he opened his mouth and told the story. By the time he'd finished, he and Cache had checked the rest of the horses and the sun was beating down from its pinnacle in the sky.

He took off his cowboy hat and wiped the sweat from his forehead. "So now I'm here."

Cache shook his head, gazing out to the pasture where the horses were. "Wow." Their eyes met, and Cache shook his hand. "I'm glad to have met you."

Carson wasn't sure what he meant by that, but something warm started in his chest. "Likewise," he said. "Now. I have to go water the llamas." He drew in a big breath. "And goat yoga starts up again in the evenings tonight."

"Yeah, tell me more about that," Cache said as they walked back to the barn to put their shoeing tools away. "Scarlett said something about cow cuddling, and I thought she was speaking Japanese."

"Cow cuddling?" Carson asked. "That I haven't heard of. But people are really getting back to the wild these days. Adele was telling me about that. They love living in the city, but they want a farm experience too."

"I guess I better look it up. I told Scarlett I would."

"Good luck," Carson said before he left the barn to get his work done over in LlamaLand.

He loved the slower pace of life. Of course, he'd never lived in a city before, so he couldn't really know if he'd like to escape the hustle and bustle of it to experience something else.

The thought of living in a big city terrified him. So many people. So much traffic. And noise. And trash. How did anyone think or feel like they mattered?

His phone buzzed in his back pocket, and he pulled it out to see he'd gotten several texts while he'd been working with Cache and the horses.

Terry.

His brother hadn't contacted him in so long, and Carson couldn't imagine that it would be good now. So he ignored that message and tapped on Adele's name instead. They'd been getting along great since he'd come back from the mapping expedition and kissed her.

She'd opened up to him more about her ex-husband, but she still hadn't invited him inside her cabin, nor told him what she was doing in there. His mind had wandered down every path he could think of, from photography and how she needed a private, dark place to develop the photos to something illicit.

But he'd never seen her take a picture with more than her phone, and she'd hired a photographer to come out during one of their goat yoga sessions and get professional pictures for the website.

So that couldn't be it. And she didn't seem like the type of woman to be doing anything illegal. No, Carson knew she wasn't doing that. She liked to cook, but he couldn't fathom why she'd need to keep a chili recipe under double lock and key.

Busy for lunch?

Not at all, he said. *I just need a few minutes to finish my chores.*

Text me when you're ready. I've got lunch for us.

His heart *ba-bumped* out an extra beat. She had lunch for them? Had she made it? Would they eat inside her cabin?

He'd also been thinking a lot about her debts and her desire to go to culinary school. He had billions. He could take care of both for her without even missing the money. His financial advisor had told him the investments Carson had opened would make six figures in the first year. That was more than enough to cover Adele's money problems.

But he'd seen her face when he'd offered. Adele would have to be dead before she'd take a dime of his money, and he didn't want that wedge between them.

He went through the gate and into LlamaLand, real-izing that he hadn't kept it as neat as Hudson did. So instead of wasting the afternoon with Adele in his arms, under the shade of a tree somewhere while they kissed and talked, he'd come back over here and get things put back together.

After all, he'd told Hudson he could manage his parts of the ranch while he was gone.

He hurried through emptying the troughs and rinsing them out. Then he set the hose to fill them, and it felt like the water was coming out in a trickle. Working quickly, he managed to clean out two stalls while filling the troughs, and then he pulled out his phone to text Adele.

All ready. I just need to wash up. Where are we eating? He looked at the words, wondering if he was being too pushy. But she'd said she had lunch for them. The natural place to eat it would be her cabin.

So he tapped *send*, hoping—and praying—that he'd done the right thing. A calm feeling blanketed him when he realized he could pray without feeling bitter or disap-pointed.

"Thank you, Lord," he said, the gratitude flowing freely now. He'd never thanked God for the financial solu-tion he'd provided Carson and Cobble Creek. Never acknowledged the Lord's hand in his escape from his father and brother.

Now, he did. Standing there on the fringes of Llama-Land, he poured his heart out to God in thanksgiving for the blessings he'd been given over the past year.

No, they had not been the specific blessings he wanted, but they were blessings nonetheless. He swallowed and sniffed as his emotions threatened to overtake him.

Then he looked at his phone when it buzzed with Adele's message.

My cabin. Knock on either door.

"Holy cow," he whispered to the screen. He looked up, his soft emotions being replaced with half excitement and half terror. "Her cabin." Then he took long strides, each one accelerating his pulse to the point where he thought he'd arrive panting and out of breath, almost over-eager to get inside and see what she was doing in there.

So he slowed down, took deep breaths, and prayed that his reaction to whatever was behind those locked doors would be precisely right.

Chapter Seventeen

Adele stirred the beef stew she'd put together that morning. In between steps, she'd sketched out her grilling week menu, as well as a whole week on using corn. The yellow vegetable was so farm-like and rustic, and she could use it in salads, as sides, and even in a main dish.

She'd made grocery lists, paid her bills for the month, and edited a video before inviting Carson to lunch.

The scent of the rolls in the oven drew her attention to them, and she pulled them out just as they were golden brown. She slathered butter over them, sure Carson would be knocking at any moment.

Her heart leapfrogged around in her chest, never settling on just one beat. She wasn't exactly sure where he was working that morning, but it had to be over in Horse Heaven or LlamaLand, because he was doing Hudson's chores.

And she didn't live that far from either.

Yet he hadn't arrived yet.

A quick glance at the clock showed that her text was only two minutes old. So maybe she was a little jumpy. Maybe her anxiety over sharing this part of herself with him was insane.

"Of course it is," she said. "It's just cooking and some video editing."

But she knew Carson didn't have any social media accounts—she may have tried looking him up a couple of weeks ago—and as she'd pondered why she didn't want him to know what went on inside this cabin, she'd realized something.

If she let him inside her physical space here, she was opening the door to her whole soul. Her whole life. There wouldn't be anything between them—no more secrets— and thus, no more barriers or defenses against falling all the way in love with him.

And that absolutely terrified her.

Knocking sounded on the back door, causing Adele to drop the tongs she'd been using to transfer the rolls from the baking sheet to a basket. They clattered on the floor with an ear-splitting metallic sound, and her pulse went ballistic.

She hurried to pick them up and toss them in the sink. Then she wiped her hands through her hair, which only reminded her she hadn't showered that morning. Swiping the straw hat she wore around the ranch off the side table, she positioned it on her head as she moved toward the back door.

It was locked, of course, and her fingers trembled as she unlatched them. With her hand still on the knob, she took in a deep breath, held it, and twisted the doorknob.

Carson stood there in all his cowboy glory—dark jeans that were actually dirty today, summer sky blue T-shirt, cowboy boots, and that delectable hat.

"Hey," he said easily as if he'd come to her cabin for lunch countless times before.

Adele gripped the doorknob tighter and backed up a step, opening the door wider than she ever had before. "Hey. Come on in."

Carson didn't move. He looked at her, and then peered over her shoulder for a quick second. "Just like that?"

"Better come in now before I freak out and slam the door."

That got him to move, and he put one foot right beside the door so it wouldn't close even if she tried to do so. He entered her personal space, his eyes locked on hers. "It's good to see you." He leaned down and kissed her, his mouth urgent and soft at the same time.

His kiss relieved some of her nerves, and she clung to him as if he was providing the very oxygen she needed to survive.

"Smells good in here," he murmured, his lips catching on hers with the words.

Adele smiled and ducked her head. "You're letting out all the air conditioning."

He entered the cabin fully and closed the door behind him. "So, you wanna give me the grand tour?" He was already looking around, and Adele couldn't blame him. She'd kept him out for so long. Yelled at him. Denied him any entry.

"Okay, so it's just a normal cabin," she said, sweeping her hand toward the living room. "Living room here. That's the front door—this place severely lacks closet space." She turned toward the kitchen. "Kitchen." Around the wall from the back door, she indicated a hall. "I have one bedroom and one bathroom down there."

"So I can wash up in there."

"Sure."

He flashed her a smile and went down the hall a few steps and into the bathroom. Adele sagged against the countertop in the kitchen, wondering why it had been such a big deal to invite him in.

"You know why," she told herself as the water started to run.

"So I don't really see anything going on here," he called.

"What do you mean?"

"Like, no dark room. No brown-paper packages." The water turned off, and a few seconds later, Carson emerged into the kitchen. "So what are you doing in here that I can't see?"

Being me, Adele thought. She bit back the words, because they felt too personal, too intimate. "Cooking," she said instead. She stepped away from the island, where her body had been blocking the hot plate. "I cook here."

"Okay," he said. "You've already told me about the cooking."

"Um, not even close." Adele pointed to the hanging rack over the island. "I film everything I cook. I make food videos and post them on the Internet." Her energy and excitement flared to life. "I'm getting a good following, and this next month, I'll be able to pay for my groceries to make the videos as well as one of my bills." He probably didn't understand how huge that was, but to Adele, making enough to pay a bill was a massive accomplishment.

"Food videos," he said, as if he'd never thought to put those two words together before. He stepped closer to the island and gazed up at the camera equipment she had there. "Lots of lights here too."

"Yeah, you want to have good light for filming," she said. "It makes the editing so much easier."

He looked at her, but his eyes seemed a little glazed over. "I know you're speaking English," he said.

"Here, let me show you." She grabbed her phone and swiped to get TastySpot open. "So I've been using a lot of my grandmother's and mother's recipes. I make theme weeks, and I cook the food, filming everything. Then I edit the video down to about fifty seconds. So you can watch me make a chicken pot pie in less than a minute."

She tilted the phone toward him, and he took it from her, his eyes wide and glued to the screen. Fifty seconds later, he looked at her. "This is amazing."

Until that moment, Adele wasn't sure how she wanted him to react. But now that he had—and done it exactly right—tears gathered in her eyes. "You think so? You don't think I'm wasting my time?"

"Adele." He glanced at the phone and then set it down on the counter. "Why would I think that?" He slipped his hands along her waist. "You can do what you want. And that looks professional. Brilliant." He glanced around and nodded toward the computer she'd set up on the dining room table. "You edit there?"

"Yes." The word caught in her throat, and she pressed her face into his chest. He smelled like horses and sweat and fabric softener, and it was everything Adele hadn't known she needed in her life.

She allowed herself a few moments of softness and emotion, and then she drew herself up to her full height. "So I'm hungry. Are you hungry?"

"Starving," he whispered, dipping his head to kiss her like he was drowning and she was his life preserver.

LATER THAT DAY, Adele moved straw around the arena as she prepped for the goat yoga session starting in a couple of hours. Lunch with Carson had been perfection. He'd said all the right things, enjoyed her stew and homemade rolls, and spent an hour listening to her as she showed him how she took her raw footage and edited it down to a bite-sized video.

He seemed interested in everything she did, and that was so foreign to her. She was trying to understand it, but she didn't, and her mind needed some open space to sort through things.

"Heya."

She glanced up to see Jeri at the fence.

"Hey, Jeri." Adele smiled at her.

"You need some help?"

"Sure," she said, though she didn't. "You're not working this afternoon?"

"We're waiting on an inspection," she said. "So I've done as much as I can do until that gets signed off." She half sighed, half exhaled as she rounded the corner and came into the arena. "Sometimes construction is nothing but waiting."

"I didn't know that," she said.

"Oh, yeah," Jeri said, picking up the pitchfork Carson usually used. "Then everything happens all at once, and we work fourteen-hour days." She shook her head, her long, dark ponytail swaying with the movement. "It can be intense."

Adele nodded and kept working. She usually didn't want to chat while she worked, but she liked Jeri, and besides, she'd just started expanding her horizons. Hadn't she?

"How's it going, living over in the Community with all the boys?" she asked.

"Oh, it's fine," Jeri said. "I'm just grateful for somewhere to lay my head."

"Yeah?" Adele watched her for a moment. Jeri was full of personality, and it seemed impossible that she could be unhappy. Now that she thought of it though, she did live at Last Chance Ranch, and that meant she hadn't had anywhere else. Or maybe it didn't.

"Yeah," Jeri said. "My general contractor license was put on probation after an accident at my last build site."

"What?" Adele asked, her heart pumping. Did Scarlett know that?

"It wasn't my fault," Jeri said. "Things happen sometimes. I followed all the procedures and the rules, but yeah." She continued moving the straw around.

Adele watched her, her initial shock wearing away. This was Last Chance Ranch. Of course Scarlett knew about the probationary license, and she'd given Jeri a chance anyway. A chance to pay her bills. A chance to have somewhere to live.

Jeri stood a few inches taller than Adele, and she had just as many pounds on her as Adele did. As they worked together, a sense of sisterhood bloomed, and Adele found the half an hour they speak together so enjoyable. Jeri talked more about her previous construction business, but she didn't detail exactly what had happened to put her license on probation.

Adele didn't ask. There was plenty of time to get the details as their friendship grew. Finally, they finished, and Adele said, "I should probably go check on the babies."

"Hey, I wanted to ask you something," Jeri said as she leaned the pitchfork against the fence.

"Sure," Adele said.

"You're not...sweet on Sawyer, are you?"

Adele's eyebrows flew up. "Sawyer?"

"Yeah, he mentioned something about taking you to lunch a couple of weeks ago, but I don't know if that ever happened." Jeri held up both of her hands, palms out, as if she'd just said something she wanted to take back. "I just wasn't sure. To me, it seemed like you and Carson were hitting it off, and...but yeah."

"Do you like Sawyer?"

"Mm, yeah," Jeri said right out loud. "Definitely. Mm-hm. A whole lot to like about that man."

Adele blinked, matched her grin to Jeri's, and then started laughing. "He's all yours, Jeri. I *am* with Carson."

I am with Carson.

She couldn't believe she'd said it so matter-of-factly. But it was true, and she didn't want it to be untrue, nor was she embarrassed by it.

Jeri laughed too, and then she said, "I like you, Adele. There's no pulling punches with you."

"Oh, I'm too old for that," she said.

"You and me both," Jeri responded. "All right. I'm going to go shower and then see if I can entice Mister Smith to ask me out."

"Good luck," Adele said, heading in the opposite direction. She went into the pasture where the goats lived, all of the babies greeting her with bleats and rubs against her legs as if they were cats.

The adults liked her too, but they approached more slowly, their crazy goat eyes scanning everything just to make sure they were safe.

"Hey, guys," she said, happiness radiating through her. No, this was more than being happy. This was joy, and she held onto it for dear life. She'd been so miserable for so long, she'd been sure she'd never feel anything this wonderful again.

Her phone bleeped, a notification sound from her social media account. She usually kept it closed or off unless she was posting, but she'd forgotten she'd opened it to show it to Carson.

And she had a new message—from Joey Dawson.

Hey, Adele. Sorry I went silent for a while there. Acquired a new building for another restaurant, and I'd love to talk to you about a position.

Her blood seemed to slow and still in her veins. "A position?" fell from her lips. What did that mean?

Joey—the celebrity chef with three New York City restaurants—sent a picture of a room that was obviously under construction. *Would love to have you out to help get the kitchen set up, if you're interested. Call me.*

His phone number stared her back in the face, and she drew in a shuddering breath.

She looked around, sure there would be an entire camera crew waiting to jump out from behind the goat barn. "Just kidding!" they'd yell.

No one jumped out from anywhere.

No one yelled anything.

Joey's number didn't disappear, and he could see that she'd seen his message.

"What do I do?" she asked the goats around her, but none of them had an answer. "Dear Lord, what do I do?"

But God didn't shake the Earth or otherwise indicate what she should do. She turned in a full circle, searching for someone to help her.

Not someone.

Carson. She wanted *Carson* to tell her what to do.

At the same time, she didn't want him to know about this chat at all, because he was obviously not a city boy, and he'd never go to New York with her.

Would he?

Chapter Eighteen

C arson sat on his back steps as the sun went down, Ted and Tony frolicking through the grass at the edge of the yard. Every so often, one of the labs would dart into the trees and bark happily.

He loved watching them enjoy themselves, his knife moving through the soft wood and creating a pile of shavings at his feet. Adele was busy tonight, making more of her cooking videos, and now that Carson knew what she was doing in her cabin, he didn't mind this time alone.

Four months ago, as the sale of the ranch was being finalized, Carson had hit a low he'd never experienced before. He'd thought he'd never get out of the darkness he existed in, and while he'd been moving at a crawl, he could feel the sunlight on his face now.

He carved with no real intention, and the wood

became an overly large spoon. Something like the spoon rest sitting on the stove at Cobble Creek.

"Not anymore," he muttered to himself. He wasn't even sure what Cobble Creek looked like anymore, if the homestead, barns, or stables would even be there anymore. It wasn't his business to know, and he'd convinced himself he didn't care.

Because he didn't.

He had a new life here in California, and he was really enjoying it. New house. New weather. New girlfriend.

Terry had texted to ask where he was, and Carson had ignored him.

The idea of buying his own ranch with his billions in the bank wiggled around in the back of his mind, but he hadn't paid much attention to it. It was kind of nice to just get up and go to work each day. No pressure. No hiring. No interviews. No worries.

The thought of going to church in the morning crossed his mind. He hadn't been in such a long time, and a sliver of guilt moved through him the same way his knife sliced through the wood in his hand, splitting the spoon rest right in half.

He sighed and looked up, his dogs still having a great time in the back yard. Maybe he could just ask Adele to go with him. She would; she went to church every week with Scarlett and Hudson.

As if summoned by his thoughts, the rumble of a truck engine met Carson's ears. Only Hudson had a truck that big, and sure enough, he pulled into his driveway a moment later.Carson stood up and went to the edge of the house just as Hudson disappeared into his cabin. He only stayed inside for a few minutes, and then he came out with Hound.

Hound.

Carson was supposed to be taking care of the dog until Monday, as well as Hudson's chores. Carson didn't see Scarlett in the front seat, and Hudson didn't waste any time backing out of his driveway and heading down the road again.

"Odd," Carson said, watching the dust lifting into the air as Hudson turned right at the end of the road to leave the ranch again. He and Scarlett were supposed to be on their weekend getaway for another two days, but something had obviously happened.

Or maybe he'd just come back for Hound and would grab dinner on his way back to the beach to meet Scarlett.

Carson whistled to his dogs and went inside his cabin with them, filling their bowls before pulling out his phone to text Adele about church in the morning.

By the time ten o'clock came the next day, Carson felt like he'd swallowed a beehive. He shouldn't have texted Adele about it so early, because his mind had been rotating around his options for hours. He could pretend to be sick. Pretend to forget he'd said he'd go. Say one of the dogs was sick.

Anything, really.

By the time Adele pulled up to his cabin, Carson stood on the front steps. But he wasn't ready for church. She got out of the sedan at the same time he went down the stairs. "I don't have anything to wear," he said.

"What do you mean?"

Carson felt like shouting. Maybe then his nerves would settle, and he'd be able to think

"You look great." Adele flashed him a smile as she moved her gaze down to his cowboy boots and back to his face.

"I'm wearing jeans and a T-shirt." He hadn't brought slacks, a tie, or white shirt. He'd thrown them all away while he packed up his whole life at Cobble Creek.

"You're a cowboy," she said. "Pastor Williams won't mind."

"I might have a collared shirt," he said. "Just a second." He took the steps two at a time back up to the porch and yanked open the front door. In his bedroom, he looked through the dozen hangers holding shirts in his closet. He did have a blue and white checkered shirt with a collar, and he whipped it down to put it on.

He couldn't believe he was even considering going to church. Especially looking like this. "My mother would die."

He stilled. His mother. His mother had left him over twenty-five years ago. He couldn't believe she was still in his mind, still influencing him at all. He supposed some lessons died hard, and this was one of them.

He'd always worn a white shirt and tie to church, even the week after the ranch had sold, and he was still begging God for a different solution.

"Carson?" Adele's voice came down the hall, and he spun away from his closet, wishing it was just as easy to get away from his thoughts.

"Coming," he said, appearing in the hall only a few steps from her.

"Why are you so nervous?" she asked, sliding her hands up his chest to finish closing the remaining buttons on his shirt. He looked down at her, finding a sense of peace in her that didn't exist inside himself.

"I haven't been to church in a while," he admitted. "I, uh, have blamed God for the loss of my ranch."

Adele nodded a few times, her gaze on his now done-up buttons. "Understandable."

"Really?" he asked. "Your ex-husband racked up thousands of dollars of debt and disappeared. Did you blame God?" He cocked his eyebrows. "Stop going to church?"

She didn't answer, which was the answer Carson needed. He fell back a step. "I don't know if I can go." He swallowed, but his throat was so dry, it scratched.

"Of course, you can," she said, reaching for him. She wrapped her fingers around his and tugged gently. "Just come sit in the back. I won't even sit by you."

"If I'm going, I'm not sitting alone." He couldn't even believe he was considering going. His heart tap danced in his chest, and he couldn't get it to stop.

"Then let's go." She tugged again, and Carson found himself going with her. He tucked in his shirt as he went, and by the time he settled in the passenger seat, he felt like he might survive just sitting in the back row.

By the time they made it to the church, the lot was full and the bell had stopped ringing. They were late, and his fantasies of going unnoticed in the back went up like smoke. When they went inside, the chapel was fairly full, and Adele guided him to a row on the side, which was still very near the back. Thankfully.

He scooted over against the wall, wiping his palms down his thighs. Adele placed herself right next to him and took his hand in hers. "There." She smiled, but she didn't look at him.

Carson took in a deep breath and tried to find his center. The core of his faith. He'd felt a few things at Last Chance Ranch over the past few weeks, and as he settled and started to listen to the pastor's voice, that same sense of peace came over him.

He didn't know Pastor Williams. Had never met the man. But he had a large personality that filled the small chapel, and his smile radiated into the corners of the room. The words he said slipped through Carson's ears, though Carson was sure they'd be good.

At that moment, though, the love and comfort flowing through him were enough.

AFTER CHURCH, he strolled with Adele along a walking path at the base of the bluff. Above them, Last Chance Ranch loomed, but he couldn't see it. No one could. People probably didn't even know it was there.

"So?" she asked. "What did you think?"

"It was...nice," he said.

"Gonna go again?"

"Probably," he said, more content than he'd felt in a long time.

They walked for a few steps in silence, and then Adele said, "I have something I want to talk to you about." She sounded serious and a little nervous, and Carson glanced at her. She didn't look at him, which only confirmed that this was a conversation he probably wouldn't like much.

"Shoot," he said casually, hoping some of his earlier anxiety over going to church had just hung around.

"Have you looked at my video account?"

"I tried," he said. "But I couldn't figure it out. I had to join, and well, I...no." Foolishness ran through him. Her cooking and videos were very important to her, and he should've tried harder before retreating back to whittling— his comfort zone. "Sorry. I'll do it this afternoon."

"It's fine," she said. "I was just wondering what you knew about it, and it seems like not much." She nudged him with her hip, and he caught the smile on her face before she glanced away. Flirting was good, so maybe this conversation would be fine.

"I'm teachable," he said.

"I'm sure you are," she said. "Anyway, it's been gaining in popularity, and I've had this big-time chef messaging me."

"Wow," Carson said.

"Yeah, he lives in New York City and has three restaurants there. Well, four now, but anyway."

He noticed that her voice had gone up in pitch and volume, and her arm had tightened on his.

"Anyway, he's opening a new restaurant, and he wants me to come help him." She laughed, but it sounded halfway maniacal. "Me. I don't even have a culinary degree. He probably doesn't even know that. He probably assumes I do, though he never asked, and I never said I did. Anyway, he wants to offer me a position. Have me come to New York and help him set up the kitchen. All of it."

Carson wasn't sure what she was saying, but he seized onto a couple of key phrases.

Offer me a position.

Come to New York.

Adele wasn't going to stay at Last Chance Ranch, keep training baby goats to jump on people's backs, and make her family recipes into videos.

"So," she said. "What do you think?"

What did he think?

He thought he was going to lose her and get his heart broken all over again. But he couldn't say that to her. So he said, "I don't know."

"You don't know?"

"No, I don't know."

"Well." She released his arm and danced in front of him. She paused, forcing him to stop walking too. She put her hands on his shoulders and flattened his already flat collar. "Would you come with me? I mean, if I go. You could—I'd want you to come with me."

Carson blinked, his mind blank. "Sure," he heard himself say. "Sure, I could go with you."

Chapter Nineteen

A dele sat with Scarlett at her island, the homemade, five-cheese macaroni and cheese bubbling away on her single burner. "So did you break up?"

"I don't know," Scarlett said, her voice somewhat of a monotone. Hudson had brought her back on Saturday sometime, and she'd been hiding in the homestead until she'd shown up at goat yoga that night. Adele had asked her if they'd broken up then, but Scarlett hadn't known that either. She said she didn't want to talk about it, and then she'd taken Gramps to dinner.

Adele had wanted to tell her about showing Carson the food videos, and Joey, and telling Carson about Joey. She had finally confessed to kissing Carson, and Scarlett had been nothing but supportive. So Adele needed to put her news beneath her tongue, and be there for her friend now.

"What did he say?"

"It happened fast," Scarlett said. "I'm pretty sure he's serious about me, but I'm just...I don't know." She sighed. "He said he already told me something, but I'm not sure what he meant."

Adele patted her hand. "You always do get a little too far inside your head."

"I know." Scarlett moaned and ducked her head, wiping her face when she lifted it again. "How long on the mac and cheese?"

"Just a few more minutes," Adele said, getting up. She crossed to the burner and took the lid off, stirring the ooey gooey, cheesy mixture around. It smelled rich and delicious, exactly how heaven better smell when she got there.

"I'm putting it over the sloppy Joe mixture. Do you want it on a bun, or just in a bowl?"

"A bun."

Adele served the sloppy Joe with mac and cheese to Scarlett with the words, "So I've been talking to Joey Dawson."

Scarlett's eyes widened, which only showed Adele the redness in them. Her best friend really had been crying most of the day. She'd already taken a bite of her sandwich, so her words were indecipherable.

Adele smiled and gestured for her to continue chewing. "He wants me to come to New York and help him set up the kitchen of his fourth restaurant. He used the word 'position.' As in, he's offered me a job."

Scarlett swallowed and wiped her mouth. "Holy mother of pearl. What are you going to do?"

"I don't know," Adele said. "Carson said he'd come with me, but I saw his face. He looked like I'd hit him with a baseball bat." It was her turn to sigh as she moved back over to her burner and filled a bowl with the sloppy Joe mixture she'd made. Then she scooped mac and cheese on top, and deliberately took a spoonful of it, showing all the gooey strings of cheese. Then she built another sandwich on the bun, cutting it with a fork.

Scarlett watched her, eating while Adele got the footage she needed. "And?" she said, the moment Adele picked up the spoon again to actually eat the bowlful of food.

"And I'm going to call Joey tomorrow," she said. "See what he really means. Ask a lot of questions." Adele put a big bite of hot food in her mouth and immediately regretted it. Her tongue and the roof of her mouth burned simultaneously, and she opened her mouth to try to cool it.

"Wow," Scarlett said. "You'd leave the west coast?"

Adele hurried to chew and swallow. "To work with an award-winning chef? I'd fly all the way around the world." Scarlett knew that, and she nodded a couple of times at the same time someone knocked on Adele's door.

"That'll be Carson." She left her bowl on the counter and dashed for the front door. She opened it to see him standing there, sans smile. "Hey. What's going on?"

"Is Scarlett here?"

"Yeah." Adele stepped back to let him in. "We're eating. There's plenty. You want some?"

"Is that a real question?" He grinned at her and moved past her without touching her. "Hey, Scarlett, uh, so I just got a text from Hudson, and he said to ask you if he could have a few weeks off." He looked between Adele and Scarlett, pure nerves in those blue eyes.

Scarlett's chin started to quiver, and Adele wrapped her arm around her friend's shoulders. "It's okay," she said softly.

"Tell him it's fine," Scarlett said.

Carson tapped on his phone, glanced up, and started for the door. "See you at class," he said, ducking outside quicker than he'd come. Adele watched him go, the spot right behind her heart hollow.

What had just happened? He'd barely looked at her, and she'd offered him food, but he'd run out. Something was definitely wrong between them, and Adele knew what it was.

New York City.

Joey Dawson.

The very food she'd been about to serve him.

Adele felt like the items around her fell away one by one, until only she remained. Her and the scent of warm milk and melted cheese. She zoned back in when she realized Scarlett was crying softly, and she went to console her.

"He'll be back," she said. "Maybe he just wanted to go

back to the beach for a bit. He worked hard to get the ranch ready for Jewel and Forever Friends." Adele kept saying different versions of the same thing, because she'd seen Hudson and Scarlett together, and she did believe they'd make it work.

They'd work it out, and make it work.

Scarlett finally left, and Adele left her food on the counter as she realized how late she was getting over to the Goat Grounds for that night's yoga class.

She enjoyed the yoga, and she liked being nearby Carson. She loved the goats, and she answered questions like a pro now. Once class ended, she and Carson usually cleaned up and got ready for the morning class, but tonight, he stood by the gate as he usually did, and stepped through it with the last guest.

He walked away without looking back and went around to the north on his way to get his dogs. They usually did that together too, cutting along the fence through the goat pasture, not going around.

"Carson," she called after him, and he paused at the corner of the fence. She approached as he turned, and her lungs felt like they needed water instead of air to function. "Hey, are you...upset with me?"

"No," he said. No smile. "I've just had a long day, and now Hudson's not going to be back for weeks, and I have a lot of work still to do." He tapped the brim of his hat in a sexy move and started walking again.

"Oh, okay," she said, turning back to the arena that

needed to be raked and fresh straw put down again. She did the work, letting her mind go wherever it wanted to. She couldn't help thinking about Joey and New York City. And Carson.

So many thoughts focused on Carson.

"He said he'd come with," she told herself. Maybe he really was just busy today. She'd go clean up her kitchen, edit her video, and stop by his place later. He liked to whittle in the evenings, or play the guitar, or throw a ball to his dogs, and he never wandered too far from his cabin.

That night, she walked over to his place, and sure enough, he sat on the front steps with his dogs at his feet. She went up the front sidewalk and joined him without saying anything.

He finally said, "Hey, beautiful."

"Oh, so I'm beautiful now." She wasn't really mad, but her tone still held part of a bite.

"Sorry about earlier," he said. "I was just frustrated over Hudson, and I didn't mean to take it out on you."

She nodded. "Apology accepted."

"I can go over to the arena in the morning and get it ready."

"I did it."

"Okay." His knife made swishing noises as he sliced it across the wood. "Did you talk to Joey today?"

"He couldn't talk today. I'm calling him after yoga in the morning." Her stomach fluttered slightly, and she wrapped her arms around her middle. "You never ate the sloppy Joe with mac and cheese. We could have that for lunch tomorrow, and I'll tell you about it."

"Deal."

Adele's worries quieted, and she laid her head against Carson's bicep while he continued to shave shards off the stick in his hand. He never did carve anything—unless a place in Adele's heart counted.

ADELE WAS TOO KEYED up from her conversation with Joey Dawson to heat up leftovers. So when Carson showed up, dirty and sweaty, she threw herself into his arms with a squeal. "He legit offered me a job. Wants me in New York in a couple of weeks."

He held onto her waist and twirled her around while she laughed. He chuckled, set her down, and said, "I'm filthy, sweetheart."

"I don't care." She backed up and held onto his shoulders. "Can you believe this? *Joey Dawson* offered me a place at his restaurant."

Carson grinned at her. "So I'll wash up while you pull up who Joey Dawson is for me." He stepped past her and into the house, sighing with the words, "Air conditioning."

She followed him inside and put two containers in the microwave, then opened her Internet browser. The words seemed piled up behind her vocal cords, and when Carson came out of the bathroom, she unleashed them.

"So he's doing a comfort food restaurant. I mean, all of his stuff is like that. He's from the South, you know? But he loves the way I combine things, and he wants larger than life portions." She clicked a couple of times and brought up his website. "See? He owns three successful restaurants in New York City already. Five star restaurants. *Michelin* star restaurants. It's incredible." She clicked on the menu. "So his fried chicken isn't just fried chicken. It's the best fried chicken on the planet."

"Impressive," he said.

"It is impressive." Giddiness pranced through her as she turned away from her computer. "Scarlett said I could go, and I really, really want you to come with me. Joey said I only need to be there for a couple of weeks, and then we'll come back here for a couple of months before the restaurant opens." She felt like she was shining, and she searched his face for any sign about how he was feeling. He wore a blank mask, so she continued.

"I mean, we'll go before the holidays and work in the kitchen with the other chefs to perfect the menu. Then it opens right after the new year."

"Leave in two weeks," he said. "Stay for two weeks. Come back for a couple of months. Then move there."

"That's right." She threw her arms around him. "So? What do you think?"

Chapter Twenty

What did he think? He thought he would never survive in New York City. He thought Adele deserved this opportunity. He didn't want to deny her anything. So he said, "I think Hudson better be back before we go, or Scarlett's going to need to hire someone else."

Adele giggled, her jolly good mood something magical. He didn't want to be the one to ruin that. He couldn't.

She stretched up and kissed him, a sloppy union of their mouths, still laughing. Then she went into the kitchen and got the food out of the microwave. He ate, contemplating what he would possibly do in New York while she was setting up the new restaurant.

It didn't matter.

This wasn't his ranch, and he had the money and

freedom to do anything he wanted. Go wherever he wanted. And he wanted to be with Adele.

He took down the calendar for goat yoga. He refunded the people who'd already paid for the classes they had to cancel. He worked from morning until night doing his chores and Hudson's chores.

Scarlett didn't seem to be in any shape to hire anyone new, but she did shift around some responsibilities, and a few of the volunteers stepped up to take over his and Hudson's chores.

The next thing Carson knew, he was loading two suitcases into the trunk of Adele's car, and they were headed into the city, their plane tickets to New York City in his back pocket. He tried to ignore the traffic. The crowds of people. The smog and dirty scent in the air.

He tried, but he failed, and by the time Adele sat down in a seat in a very busy terminal, his nerves felt like someone had fed them to a chainsaw. He flashed her a smile and stuck his headphones in his ears—anything to isolate himself a little bit.

Thankfully, Adele seemed quite content to exist inside her head too, and they spent the day making connecting flights, eating on the go, and then sharing a cab to the hotel Joey had said would be ideal for their visit to the city.

Carson had paid for it—insisted, and maybe even threatened not to go with Adele if she didn't let him pay for their hotel rooms—and it was nicer than anywhere Carson had ever lived.

"Dinner?" Adele asked when they made it to the twenty-second floor.

"Can we order in?"

"I'll call room service and knock when it's here," she said with a smile.

Room service. Carson had no idea what that entailed, and he was too tired to think about it. Inside his own room, he let the door close and he leaned against it, a long sigh hissing from his mouth.

He left his suitcase right where it was, a few feet inside the door, and walked over to the bed. Nothing about the room was big, including the bed. Outside the window, he did take a moment to enjoy the view of the city.

He stood there for a moment, feeling very small and very insignificant. Not that Carson had ever claimed much importance in this world. It was very easy to feel tiny under the huge sky in Montana. And lost driving away from it. And like a speck of dust among the hubbub and activity and people of New York City.

After removing his boots, he collapsed onto the bed and stacked three pillows under his head, relishing the release of pain when he closed his eyes. He'd wake up when Adele knocked with dinner.

The next time he opened his eyes, everything was pitch black and a chill played against his skin. A groan came out of his mouth as he sat up, blinking, trying to figure out where he was.

The clock on the table beside the bed—he was in the

hotel in the city—said it was almost two o'clock in the morning, and his phone flashed with a blue light. Adele's text said, *I couldn't get you to answer the door. You're a heavy sleeper, country boy. ;)*

His lips curled up softly at her words. At the very thought of her, and Carson wondered if this was what love felt like. A softness in his heart he'd never felt before and didn't know how to categorize. Traveling all the way across the country so she could have the thing she wanted.

I have dinner when you wake up.

He finished reading her string of texts and got up to go to the bathroom. He wasn't going to go next door this late at night—or early in the morning, depending on how he looked at it—to get whatever she'd ordered for him hours ago.

Sure, his stomach growled, but he'd survive.

How he made it to morning, he wasn't sure. It felt like an act of God, as Carson never really fell back asleep after changing into his pajamas and closing the curtains against the bright city lights of Times Square.

By the time Adele knocked on his door, looking fresh and fabulous, Carson felt ready to fly back home.

Home.

He wasn't entirely sure where home was at the moment, but he knew it wasn't here in New York City.

But maybe it was with Adele Woodruff. He was so confused, and he didn't know what to think.

"Hey, cowboy," she said. "You crashed last night."

"Yeah, sorry about that."

"I got you a burger and fries, but I don't think they'll be good this morning."

"Nope. Just toss them. We can go to breakfast."

"We're meeting Joey and his wife for breakfast, remember?"

"Oh, of course." Carson gave himself a mental shake, wishing he'd made a few notes of their itinerary. Well, really, *Adele's* itinerary. "Do we have time for coffee?"

"There's always time for coffee." She turned and started down the hall, and Carson dashed back to the TV stand and grabbed his wallet and keycard. When he joined her in the hall, he took her hand in his.

"Sorry about the food. I hope it wasn't too much."

"Oh, you paid for it. So it's fine." She laughed, the sound glorious and dancing through his mind.

Energy pulsed off the street when Carson stepped outside, and it invigorated something inside him. Strangely enough, the peace and quiet on the ranch did the same thing. So maybe the city had a personality too, one that could speak to him the same way open fields and mountains could.

"I think there's a coffee shop down here," she said, leading him to the left. Carson felt very out of place in his cowboy hat and boots, but nobody stared at him. Everything around him seemed to loom stories and stories above him, and he couldn't see a store anywhere.

He was just about to say something when Adele

turned to go through a door. A door to the coffee shop. He hadn't even seen it. The scent of coffee and chocolate hit him, making his stomach practically riot.

He should've known there would be a line, but it still surprised him to have to wait behind four other people.

"Is this great?" Adele bubbled. "This place is so cute. Look at those dog biscuits." She waggled her fingers at a woman carrying a little white dog in her purse.

Carson didn't know where to look, so he stuck close to Adele and let her order for him. Once they made it back to the sidewalk, Carson felt like he could breathe again. They strolled easily now, and before he knew it, Adele stood in front of another man and woman, shaking both of their hands.

"This is my boyfriend, Carson Chatworth," she said, stepping back so Carson could shake hands.

"Joey Dawson," the man said as they shook. He had almost black hair and a goatee to match. His eyes were as dark as the coffee Carson drank, but they sparkled like diamonds. His wife—Yvonne—had long, wavy hair in a variety of blondes and browns, none of them real. She smiled at him with her mouth and her blue eyes, but she was the kind of woman that struck fear right between Carson's ribs.

He shook her hand anyway, feeling very out of place. He wasn't the type to stand on the street, visiting with friends, and yet there he was.

"So should we go over?" Joey asked, and Adele readily

agreed. They walked a couple of blocks to the new restaurant, Adele chattering away about recipes and cuts of beef. Carson followed along like a puppy desperate for attention. He'd done the same thing at Last Chance Ranch too, but the difference was, he didn't mind it there.

Joey stood just inside the door and started gesturing to corners and walls, talking about tabletops and bars and other things Carson wasn't sure of. They moved into the kitchen, and he went to follow them, noticing that Yvonne didn't. She'd sat at a chair, her coffee cup in one hand and her phone in the other.

"You're not going back?" he asked.

She looked up from her phone. "I've been here a dozen times." She faked a yawn. "It's a big empty room, just like this one."

Carson looked to the doorway Adele had gone through and back to Yvonne. "Can I join you?"

"Be my guest. They'll be in there for a while, talking about ovens and walk-ins. It's not terribly exciting."

"I can't imagine it would be." Carson sat down in the chair opposite her. "What do you do?"

"I manage Joey's career." She flashed a pink-lipped smile at him. "His appearances, his filming schedule, meetings like this, all of it."

Carson nodded like he understood what that meant, but in reality, he had no idea. He looked down at his phone in tandem with Yvonne, but she had something to do on her device. He texted and called, but he didn't do anything else. No social media to check. No games to play. Just another way he didn't fit in with this society.

His pulse pinched and it felt like someone had wrapped a rubber band around his chest and kept winding it tighter and tighter. As the minutes stretched, he wondered how long he needed to sit here and wait.

He told himself to be patient, that he'd come to New York City to support Adele in this dream. He'd had plenty of opportunities over the past few weeks to tell Adele he didn't want to come. That he'd never traveled farther east than the Rocky Mountains, and that he didn't like cities.

Surely she knew, though. It wasn't like he'd kept any of his personality back from her.

His thoughts moved to Texas. He remembered Cache telling him his father and brother took their cattle to Shiloh Ridge in Texas, and he wondered if he should go visit the ranch.

He dismissed the idea. He didn't need another job. He had one at— His thoughts stalled. He hadn't exactly quit his job at Last Chance Ranch, but he'd told Scarlett he'd be in and out with Adele.

"Excuse me," he said, standing up. Yvonne didn't say anything, barely looked up at him as he strode away. He practically burst out of the space, pulling in a deep breath of morning air. The sun was already hot here in the city, but he didn't care. He could breathe out here, and that was all that mattered.

A WEEK LATER, Carson didn't get coffee with Adele. They didn't hold hands as they walked down the city streets to what would become the new restaurant. They hadn't done anything together that they'd talked about. No visit to the Statue of the Liberty. No city tour buses pointing out all the sights to see. No Chinatown. No Broadway plays.

Carson had spent most of his time in the hotel room, climbing the walls. Or listening to Adele gush about Joey and the opportunity she had to cook for him. If she knew he was dying a slow death, she didn't acknowledge it.

Hudson had texted him to find out why he wasn't at the ranch, so he knew Hudson and Scarlett had made up. Which was great. Just great. He felt like his relationship was unraveling one string at a time, no matter how he tried to grab onto the end of it and hold it tight.

Chapter Twenty-One

Adele could hardly sleep while in New York City, and it had nothing to do with the city traffic, the sirens in the middle of the night, or loud people coming in late to the room next door. Her excitement kept her brain whirring until the wee hours of the morning, and she'd drawn no less than four maps of the kitchen at the restaurant down the street.

Joey's After Hours.

He'd told her the name yesterday, shown her the sign he'd ordered, and consulted her on the layout and color of the menu. *Consulted* her.

Adele hadn't really been consulted about much in her life, and it sure was nice to think she had thoughts and opinions that someone else cared about.

She didn't need sleep. The coffee shop down the street had delicious cappuccinos and lattes, and she hadn't held back on sampling all the good food the city had to offer either. Carson had stopped coming with her to the restaurant, and a twinge of guilt hit her that they hadn't done any of the touristy things she'd promised they would.

"We'll be living here soon," she whispered to herself. They'd have plenty of time to see the Empire State Building and Central Park once they moved here permanently.

The thought put fear in her mind, and that kept her awake now. If she and Carson were going to move across the country together, that meant their relationship was serious. And could she admit that it was?

She'd only known him for a couple of months, and she wasn't wearing his ring. They hadn't even talked about marriage. Or where they'd live once they came back to New York City for good.

He'd been out looking at neighborhoods while she'd been developing recipes in one of Joey's functioning kitchens. A real, restaurant kitchen. Thoughts of Carson disappeared behind the way her life had changed completely in the last couple of weeks.

Tomorrow was her last day in the city, and she'd already tied up all the loose ends with Joey and the restaurant. She and Carson had planned a late breakfast before they left for the airport and headed back to California.

By the time she woke up—so she did sleep a little bit—packed, and made it next door, Carson's room was empty.

At least he wasn't answering her knocking. She turned in a circle in the hall and pulled her phone out of her pocket.

She did have a text from him, though she'd just looked at her phone, and she hadn't seen it. "Strange," she muttered as she swiped to open it.

I'm downstairs, it read. Nothing else.

Adele reached for her bag and continued down the hall, irritation rising within her. Why hadn't he come next door and gotten her before he'd just left?

In the lobby, Carson sat on the couch, his head leaned back and his eyes closed. "Hey," she said when she arrived next to him.

He opened his eyes, and it took a moment for him to focus on her. "There you are."

"Here I am? Yes, here I am."

Carson's expression hardened, and he stood. "I knocked, but you didn't answer. I thought maybe you'd come down here for coffee, but I didn't see you."

"I just knocked on your door."

"Why would you do that?"

"We're supposed to go to breakfast on our way to the airport."

"Yeah," he said. "Forty minutes ago." He held up his phone as if she could see the clock on it.

"What? No." She yanked her own phone out of her pocket. "We agreed to meet and leave at nine...." Her brain caught up to her mouth when she saw that it was almost nine-forty-five, and her memory jiggled enough to tell her they'd agreed to meet at nine.

Nine. Not nine-thirty.

Her anger leaked out of her, replaced instead with embarrassment. "I'm sorry," she said.

"Let's just go," he said. "I can't wait to get back to the ranch." He grabbed his bag and hers and started for the doorway, leaving her to stare after him. Her heart fell down to the bottom of her feet and rebounded to the back of her throat. Pain radiated through her with the strength of his words.

I can't wait to get back to the ranch.

He wasn't happy here, and Adele hadn't even seen it. How had she missed it?

Sure, he'd been a little quieter while they'd been here, but Carson had always been a man of few words. She'd been busy, but he'd said he didn't mind.

Adele realized that he'd reached the doors without looking back once. She hurried after him and caught him right as a cab pulled up to the curb. The driver and Carson got the bags in the back, and he slid into the car with the words, "JFK, please."

"We're not going to breakfast?"

"I don't think we have time," he said, adjusting his hat.

Her nerves pranced around "What did you mean back there?" she asked.

"About what?"

"That you can't wait to get back to the ranch."

"That I can't wait to get back to the ranch." Carson kept his gaze out the window.

Adele didn't know what else to say, and the drive to the airport didn't seem to take long at all. After that, the time dragged on and on. The line at security took forever, and since they were earlier than she'd anticipated, they sat at the gate forever.

Too late for breakfast, but too early for the airport. The whole day felt like a bust, and she wanted to crawl back into bed.

No, she didn't want to go back to the ranch.

But go back she did. All the way across the country, out of the city, and past the robot mailbox that marked the entrance to Last Chance Ranch.

She dropped Carson off at his house, where Hudson waited on the porch with Tony and Ted.

"Hey," Carson said, real happiness in his voice as he walked away from the car. The dogs barked and ran down the steps to meet him. Carson released his suitcase and bent down to scrub them, letting them lick his face hello, their tails going around like whips.

Hudson joined them, and the two men shook hands. Adele watched through the windshield, removed from the scene and yet still fully a part of it.

"When did you get back?" Carson asked.

"Oh, just before my birthday." His gaze wandered to Adele, and she flipped the car into reverse and pulled out of the driveway. She commanded herself not to look back, and she succeeded.

Her cabin felt lonely and empty, and she dragged her bag down the hall and into the bedroom. She collapsed into bed, fully clothed, and fell asleep almost instantly.

HER LIFE WENT BACK to the country kind of normal she'd made for herself at Last Chance Ranch. She worked with the goats, who seemed a bit stand-offish when she first went back. Scarlett had hired someone to oversee the animal adoptions at the ranch, and Amber Haws had been running the goat yoga, too.

The blonde had long, gorgeous waves of hair, and big brown eyes that smiled all the time. The goats loved her, and Adele felt slightly abandoned by these babies she'd raised and trained.

But they warmed up to her quickly, despite the fact that she wasn't really running the program anymore. She didn't lead the yoga. She'd taken over Carson's job of standing at the gate and checking people off as they came in.

She watched while a trained instructor from town did the session, then she and Amber cleaned up and got ready for the next session.

Adele did enjoy getting back to her videos. She'd been inspired by the recipe creation in the city, and she did a week themed around appetizers, and one around soups before she admitted to herself that things between her and Carson were cracked.

They saw each other, but the passion in their kisses wasn't nearly the same, and he wouldn't say anything about how he was feeling. One day near the end of August, she wandered down the road toward the part of the ranch where the horses, llamas, and pigs lived.

Carson spent most of his days there now, only stopping by her place a couple of times a week for lunch. Of course, Scarlett had hired several more people, one of which included a woman who ran the marketing side of the ranch and happened to enjoy feeding a crowd.

Karla Jenkins had taken up residence in the cabin beside Adele's, and the white tables they'd set up for their Fourth of July picnic remained against that cabin perpetually now. She sent group texts to let everyone on the ranch know if lunch would be served that day, and what the menu was.

Adele wasn't jealous of her exactly. She simply felt like maybe she'd been replaced—in more ways than one. Scarlett didn't need her as much anymore, not with her relationship with Hudson doing so well, not to mention all the new people on the ranch for company.

"Hey," she said to Hudson when she found him near the pasture.

"Hey, Adele." He smiled at her and continued doing something with a saddle to make it shine.

"Have you seen Carson?"

"Yeah, he's over in Piggy Paradise today," he said. "It's rotation day."

Adele didn't know what that meant, but she nodded, smiled, and left Hudson to his saddle. Piggy Paradise was several hundred yards past the stables, and Adele took her time getting there.

She had a feeling her conversation with Carson wasn't going to end the way she wanted it to. She found him pushing on the hind end of a huge potbellied pig while Sawyer pulled on a leash he'd put around the pig's head.

The animal wasn't moving, and it didn't seem that the two cowboys, as big and strong as they were, could do anything about it.

She watched for a few more seconds, because it was funny, and then Sawyer caught sight of her. He nodded toward her, and Carson looked over his shoulder. He gave up trying to budge the pig, wiped his hands—though that didn't do anything to improve the cleanliness of them—and walked over to her.

"Hey," he said over the fence, a quick smile gracing his face.

"Hey." She sighed and put her arms up on the top rung of the fence. "How's it going out here?"

"Not well. That pig is the most stubborn thing I've ever encountered." He took his hat off and wiped his hair back.

"You need a haircut," she teased, reaching up and

touching the long ends of his hair before he re-seated his hat.

"Are you volunteering?" He hadn't flirted with her for so long, Adele wasn't sure what was happening for a moment.

"Heavens, no," she said. "I knew a lot of hairdressers, but I was not one of them."

He smiled and leaned against the fence too, bending down to kiss her. She held onto the feeling rushing through her, because it felt like the first time in a while that he actually wanted to be with her.

Her heart pinched, and she wondered how in the world she could leave him here in California when she went back to New York City.

In that moment, she knew she'd be going and he wouldn't.

She pulled away but stayed tipped up on her toes, in his personal space. "You're not going to come to New York with me when I go, are you?"

"No, Adele," he whispered, the tip of his nose running up her cheek before he backed up further.

She sighed and settled flat on her feet. Her mind was blank, and her chest felt like someone had hollowed it out and poured lemon juice inside.

"So I guess that's it," she said. "Are we broken up, then?"

"I don't know, Adele." He looked at her, right at her. "I sure do like you, but that city suffocated me. I can't...I just...can't go back there with you." He held up both hands and backed up a couple of steps. "I'm so sorry."

"It's okay," she murmured, though it certainly wasn't okay. Her heart wailed as it cracked, and there was absolutely nothing she could do about it.

Chapter Twenty-Two

C arson deliberately stayed home the day Adele was set to leave Last Chance Ranch. Scarlett and Hudson had told him she'd moved up her departure date, and he'd asked if he could just stay home so he wouldn't accidentally run into her.

Since their last kiss two weeks ago, he'd seen her a few times and it had been seven shades of awkward each time. Worse than the yelling matches in the parking lot and outside her cabin, because now he knew her. Now he couldn't have her, and he knew it.

He wondered if Last Chance Ranch was where he was supposed to be. The thought of leaving this pretty piece of country for the unknown had his stomach in knots, but he wasn't sure he could stay here after Adele left.

But that meant he'd have to leave tomorrow, and he had nowhere to go.

He'd had friends in Montana, and a couple of them had offered him a place on their ranch. But Carson hadn't been able to stay in the state if he wasn't at Cobble Creek. But now, he wondered if he could go back.

He'd been going to church, and trying to find his way back to God, and the thought didn't quite sit right in his chest and mind. So Montana was out.

Where else could he go?

"Ho!" A voice sounded outside his house, in a place it shouldn't have been—along the tree line. He moved quickly to the back door and pulled it open to see Cache waving his hat after a couple of errant cows that had obviously gotten out.

Carson hurried down the steps and dashed across his lawn. "Where do you need me?" he called, drawing Cache's attention.

"On the right flank," he said, and Carson ran behind him, fanning out to the right, dodging trees and hoping he didn't go down on a hidden branch. He headed the cows—four of them—and turned them back toward the cabins in the Community, where Cache had found more reinforcements. Hudson, David, and Jeri were there with ropes, and they made short work of the errant dairy cows.

"They love grass," Cache said, panting between words. "They'll eat and eat until they die. Stupid cows."

He slapped one affectionately on the rump. "Thanks, everyone."

Carson almost started walking over to the cattle pasture with Cache, then he realized he couldn't get that close to the homestead or Adele's cabin. Her flight wasn't until that evening, and she was cleaning her cabin out that day. Taking things to storage, if he'd heard right.

His heart flipped around backward, because he should be helping her. That would be the Christlike thing to do. Swallow his pride and his feelings and go help her. He kept walking with Cache, who started chuckling.

"You're good with the cows," he said.

"Yeah, well, I've had a few get out on me too." He couldn't help the way his gaze wandered toward Adele's cabin. An idea hit him right in the middle of his brain. "Hey, do you think they need help at Shiloh Ridge Ranch?"

"Shiloh Ridge?" Cache asked. "I have no idea. Why?"

"I'm...I don't think I can stay here," he said, catching a glimpse of Adele's house. "Me and Adele...you know."

"Ah, I see. Well, I can call my brother tonight. Or right now." He kept a tight grip on the ropes leading the cows and dug in his pocket for his phone.

"Oh, you don't need to—"

"Already dialing." Cache gave him a big smile, and a moment later, he said, "Hey, Leo, it's your favorite little bro." He laughed, and Carson heard chuckles on the other end of the line too.

They talked for a few minutes, and then Cache said, "Hey, what's the personnel like there at the ranch right now?" There was a healthy pause before Cache spoke again. "Yeah, I got a guy looking for something. He's really experienced. Owned a cattle ranch in Montana." Cache cut him a look, and Carson tried to smile. But he hadn't been doing a whole lot of that recently, and it felt strange on his face.

"So I can give him Bear's number? All right, bro. Gotta go." Cache hung up a moment later, and said, "I've got a name and number for you." They walked along the road, the gate only a few yards away now. "I'm bummed you'll be leaving. I mean, I get it. But yeah."

"Me too," Carson said, the first measure of sadness pulling through him as he moved forward to open the gate so Cache could walk the dairy cows back where they belonged. "But I'm just not sure this is where I'm supposed to be."

"Well, you can call Bear Glover. Find out if Shiloh Ridge is where you want to be."

Carson didn't bother correcting Cache. It wasn't about what he wanted anymore. He knew that now. For some reason, God hadn't wanted him to have Cobble Creek. Maybe he was supposed to come here and meet Adele Woodruff. Maybe he wasn't. Since things hadn't worked out with her, he couldn't fathom why God would've wanted him here just to get his still-bruised heart broken all over again.

He expected the same crushing anger and guilt to hit him, but it didn't. He knew now that God wasn't out to punish him or make his life more difficult.

But maybe God could give him a place to be at Shiloh Ridge in Texas.

TEN DAYS LATER, Carson drove through the same farmland that he'd loved in Montana. Yes, these acres were hundreds of miles further south, but they reminded him so much of everything he loved that he already felt calm and hopeful about his decision to leave Last Chance Ranch and try Shiloh Ridge.

The ranch sat only a few minutes outside of the picturesque town of Three Rivers, and he liked that he wouldn't have to drive far for groceries and socialization. Shiloh Ridge was a dairy farm, which was something Carson didn't have a whole lot of experience with. But they had eight thousand head of cattle that needed tending to, and four vacancies for cowboys.

Bear Glover had hired him over the phone a week ago, and Carson had finished up his responsibilities, hugged Scarlett while she cried and begged him to stay, told him Adele would come back to him, and then driven across several states to be here.

He took a deep breath, his lungs expanding fully for the first time since Adele had left California. "Help me feel...help me know what to do." He turned off the truck and got out of it, walking toward a big building that looked like a ski lodge but was clearly the administration building.

The good, earthy scent of cows and hay and rolling Texas hills met his nose, and Carson smiled. The log cabin had a tall set of stairs he took one at a time, deliberately. Once inside, he couldn't turn back.

He opened the door and went inside, expecting to see cowboys everywhere. But the building that he could see was empty. A desk sat a few feet away, but it too sat empty. Someone was supposed to be there, but there was a tented piece of paper that said, "In the kitchen. Wait or come on back."

Carson was tired of waiting, so he went on back. It was easy enough to find the kitchen, because the scent of marinara sauce drew him in the right direction. "Hey," he said to the woman stirring something on the stove. "The sign said come on back."

A woman turned, and she was easily his mother's age —if he'd seen his mother lately. "Oh, you must be Carson Chatworth." She left the wooden spoon in the pot and bustled over to him, her dark hair swinging a little. Her smile warmed his heart, and surprise darted through him when she pulled him right into a hug.

"Ma, you can't hug all the new hires," a man behind him said, and the woman released Carson.

"Yes, I can," she said. "And I made spaghetti and meatballs too. Come on. Come in. The other boys will be in soon."

Carson looked at the other man, finding the same sloped nose and dark hair poking out from under his cowboy hat. He had dark eyes and a face full of hair. He smiled widely, his eyes shining. "I'm Bear."

"Carson."

"So apparently, we're eating lunch first. Then I'll show you your cabin and we'll talk about your job duties."

"Sounds great," Carson said as his stomach growled. Spaghetti and meatballs sounded delicious about now. He watched Bear's mother get out real plates and pull forks from a drawer.

"My mother," Bear said. "She hugs without even introducing herself. Her name's Trudy. She loves taking care of all the farm hands." He shook his head as the first man came into the room. "I'm an only child, so it feeds her desire to take care of everyone."

"You must be the reason we're getting fed today." The cowboy grinned and pushed past Carson and Bear.

"That's Steven," he said, and several more arrived. Carson got lost in all the names and faces, and he decided he had plenty of time to meet everyone and get to know them.

The very thought made him tired. He didn't want to meet two dozen new people, start a new job at a new ranch, live in a tiny cabin by himself.

Problem was, he didn't know what else to do. Or where else to go.

New York City, his mind whispered, but he absolutely couldn't go back there. He hadn't heard from Adele since she left, and he wasn't going to text her. He'd told her he couldn't go with her, and she'd chosen to go anyway.

So he put his head down. He unpacked his boxes in the tiny cabin. Reported for work the next morning. Met new people and tried to remember their names.

Days passed and became weeks, which became a month and then two. It snowed a skiff in the hills in the Texas panhandle, and the other farm hands complained about the cold and mud. Not Carson. He loved it, because it reminded him of home.

Home.

He still wasn't sure where home was for him, but for right now it was Shiloh Ridge Ranch. His thoughts zipped over to the people he knew at Last Chance Ranch, the way they often did. He wasn't sure if that was home either, but he knew he'd left part of his heart there.

Thankfully, Scarlett and Hudson were getting married in April, and he'd already gotten the time off to go. He wondered if Adele would be there, if she was still living and cooking in New York City, or if she'd landed somewhere else. Where, he wasn't sure. He could probably check her cooking video social media page and find out, but he still hadn't joined it. After all, he had Trudy cooking most of his meals these days, and he had no need to watch sixty-second clips of how to make gourmet food.

But he sure did want to see those videos, if only to remind himself of how much he'd enjoyed his time with Adele.

A keen sense of missing seemed to accompany him to every chore, every church meeting, every cold evening with his dogs.

And his last prayer before he felt asleep each night was *Adele. Help Adele to be happy.*

Chapter Twenty-Three

Adele had been tired before, but working as a chef—and not even the executive chef—in a busy New York City restaurant brought a whole new level of exhaustion into her life. When she wasn't at the restaurant, which was most of the time, honestly, she was sleeping in her studio apartment on a ratty couch. No bed. The couch would convert into one, but she hadn't had time to go buy a mattress.

She had some money now to do that, but no time.

At Last Chance Ranch, she'd had nothing but time. Time with her baby goats. Time to cook her family recipes. Time to hold hands and stroll around the ranch with Carson.

She tried to push the handsome cowboy out of her mind, but he never went far, and never for very long. She cooked for people in costume. She cooked for people who didn't want to cook for themselves on Thanksgiving.

As Christmas approached, and Mother Nature brought rain, hail, and snow to the city, Adele wondered— not for the first time—what in the world she was doing. It had always been warm in Savannah, and the weather couldn't be better in California.

Then she'd think that she couldn't believe she was thinking about the weather. The *weather*, of all things. Her life had been reduced to hating the weather, sleeping on a couch, and cooking shrimp stackers for hours on end.

"Shrimp app," Billy, the expeditor, called. "Four. Beet salad, two."

"Shrimp, four," Adele called out, setting the pans she needed on the stove. She tossed butter into each of them, then added a spoonful of garlic to flavor it. Three shrimp went in each pan with a satisfying sizzle. She tossed and flipped them as they went from translucent to opaque, and she sprinkled the spice mixture the executive chef—Alexa —had put together. The shrimp turned a brighter shade of red, and she grabbed the long toothpicks she used just for this appetizer. Stab, stab, stab, and one stacker was done.

"One minute on stackers," she called.

"Beet salad in one," the line cook down the row called.

"Where's the dessert for table thirty-four?" Billy asked. "I've got two tiramisu and two pumpkin cheesecake going on ten minutes."

"Teresa stepped out," someone said as Adele stacked

her third appetizer.

"Out?" Billy called. "Who can get me these desserts?"

"I can," Adele called, putting her last appetizer on the plate. She sprinkled parsley over them, the green and red making this dish extra festive. She wiped the plates and set them in the window. "Two tiramisu. Two pumpkin cheesecake."

"Thanks, Adele."

Her feet hated her. She'd never sweated so much. But she'd wanted this experience more than anything, and she refused to feel sorry for herself. She was the only one in the kitchen who didn't have a culinary degree. Had never even been to culinary school. So if her feet hurt a little and she wasn't sleeping as much as she used to, so what?

So what?

The words bounced around inside her head as she swirled the cheesecake with whipped cream and set the two desserts in the window. Her appetizers went out, and a flash of pride hit her.

In the beginning, she'd felt this level of pride for her whole shift. Now, months later, it came and went, usually like lightning. Striking one moment and disappearing the next.

She'd no sooner set the cheesecake in the window and a waiter whisked the desserts off with a look like she'd done something wrong when Joey Dawson himself breezed into the kitchen.

"Adele," he said, putting his arm around her shoulders.

"Just the chef I wanted to see."

"Hey," she said with a smile. "What's up?" She'd learned to get him right to the heart of the business, or hours could be wasted.

"Have you seen the new videos on TastySpot?"

Yes, she had. And no, she wasn't happy about them. The flashy, high-cost foods featured in the videos didn't fit her brand. She wasn't sure who was making them, or where the recipes were coming from, but she wished it was still her. Still her recipes and ideas. Her theme weeks. But Joey had gotten rid of all of that, and instead turned the account into something more commercial.

The followers had doubled and then tripled, but the comments weren't nearly as personal. No one was actually making the food in the videos, the way they used to when she'd first started.

"Yeah, I've seen it," she said, hoping she could keep the emotion out of her voice.

"And?" he asked, looking at a plate as it left the kitchen. "Billy, what was that?"

"Red snapper on the menu tonight," Billy said without looking up from a ticket.

"Huh," Joey said. "Is that part of our menu?" He looked at Adele, who nodded.

"Yeah," she said. "It's seafood night." His name got people in the doors, but his executive chef really ran the place. Oh, and Billy.

"Shrimp app," Billy said, looking at her. "Three."

"Shrimp, three," she said and deftly moved away from Joey and back in front of the stove that had pulled her away from her best friend, the ranch, her goats, and Carson.

MONTHS LATER, Adele clutched the steering wheel as she drove the rental car up the road toward Last Chance Ranch. The robot mailbox had obviously been decked out in the proper attire for Scarlett's and Hudson's nuptials, as it now wore a bow tie and someone had painted white wedding bells on the glass portion of his boxy chest.

Adele smiled at Prime, the robot that Scarlett's brother had named when they were kids, coming to visit the ranch and their grandparents. Scarlett had told Adele that story so many times, she almost felt like she'd been there when the robot was named.

As soon as she passed Prime, her nerves returned in full force. They'd been assaulting her for hours now, on her long journey across the country.

Scarlett had told her that Carson had left shortly after Adele had, so she knew he didn't live here anymore. But Scarlett and Hudson had invited him to the wedding, of course, and he'd RSVP'ed that he'd be there.

Which meant Adele was going to have to see him. He held such a prominent place in her mind and heart that she wondered if she'd even recognize him in real life. The picture of him in her mind might be different than who he was now, and she constantly reminded herself of that as she drove down the lane and parked in the driveway at the homestead.

Instead of going straight inside though, she turned and faced the Goat Grounds, only to be met with the sight of dozens of cows across the street in the pasture where her goats used to be. Things had definitely changed around here.

She breathed, and it was easier here than in New York, where a freak April snowstorm had practically shut down the city. She liked the easy way of life here, the way the sun shone down on everything equally, how there was no one yelling at her for a time status on a bowl of polenta or a salad with more ingredients than she had fingers and toes.

After crossing the street, she continued toward the goat yoga arena, which now boasted a huge sign with those words arching across the entrance. She went in, noting the straw was all ready for the next session. The goats had been moved into another pasture, this one sectioned off from the cattle.

"Hey, babies," she said as she stepped inside. The littler goats came over, but they didn't react to her the same way her ice cream flavored animals had. Of course, there were new babies working the goat yoga sessions now, and they were the friendliest with her. They probably thought she had graham crackers in her pockets.

She bent down and looked into the crazy eyes of the nearest goat. "What's your name, huh?" she asked. "I'm going to call you Peaches." Yes, if these were her goats, they'd all have fruit names. Fuji, Melon, Pineapple.

She smiled at her own cleverness and let her fingers trail along the back of another baby goat. Her phone buzzed out Scarlett's notification sound, and Adele sighed. It was time to go inside, get zipped and strapped into a frilly dress, and attend her best friend's wedding.

Adele hesitated just before she knocked on the front door of the homestead, pushing it open as he called, "Hello? Scarlett?"

Shrieks ensued, and Adele got caught up in the hugging and jumping up and down and gushing over her best friend's new hair color and cut. She held onto Scarlett for longer than comfortable, her emotions spiraling around inside her.

"Oh, honey," Scarlett whispered, holding her tight again. "Why don't you just come back? I didn't give your cabin away."

Adele backed up and swiped at her eyes. "I'm fine. I'm just so happy for you." And she *was* thrilled for Scarlett. She loved that her best friend had found a place to be, and a man to love and be loved by, and she was absolutely glowing.

She couldn't help wanting that for herself, could she? Did that make her a bad person, to want the joy radiating from Scarlett's face for herself?

She smiled, swiped one more time at her eyes, and said, "You got my new dress size, right?" She'd lost quite a bit of weight when she'd been working on the ranch, but she'd gained it all back in the city. Yes, she sweated through most of her shifts, but then she ate bar food in the middle of the night, did no other exercise, and slept poorly the rest of the time.

"I got it right here." Scarlett beamed at her and dashed down the hall. "Come try it on."

Adele glanced at the two other women in the room— Jeri and Amber—but she didn't stay to chat. She waved at them, wishing they weren't better friends with Scarlett than she was, and went down the hall into Scarlett's bedroom.

"I'm sorry," she said immediately, bringing the door closed behind her. "I've been a terrible friend."

"You have not." Scarlett turned, something hideously blue in her hand.

"Tell me that's not the dress."

"I can't tell you that," she singsonged. "Now, come put this on. It's *so* pretty."

Adele and Scarlett had different definitions of pretty, clearly, but Adele did as her friend wanted. She let Scarlett zip her and tug on the sleeves, tuck something into the neck, and then stand back. "See?"

Adele saw, and what she did, she didn't like. She had too much sitting on certain curves, and her short hair wasn't doing her any favors with the scooping neckline.

She smoothed her hands down her stomach, but that didn't make it any smaller.

Scarlett hugged her from behind. "You're so pretty. Thank you for coming."

Adele met her eyes in the mirror. "Of course I'd be here. I wouldn't miss it."

"It's just that...you know. Carson's here."

"We're both adults," Adele managed to squeeze out of her too-tight throat. At least she hoped they were both adults. She was determined to sit on the side, bouquet in her hands, and keep her eyes on the happy couple. She could do that. She could.

"Wow, I think you're handling this really well," Scarlett said.

"Why wouldn't I be?" Adele asked, finally turning to look at Scarlett.

"Adele, you're in the wedding party."

"Yeah," she said, not getting it.

"So is Carson."

Horror struck Adele in the chest. She tried to shake it off. "It's fine. I'll be fine." So she might have to be close to him for a few minutes while they walked down the aisle ahead of Scarlett and Hudson. She'd have to smell his cologne. It would be okay. She could handle it.

The following day, the tent and chairs were set up. The trees were flowering with pink blossoms, just the way Scarlett wanted. The barn had been cleaned and decorated for the reception, dinner, and dancing.

Adele waited until the last minute to leave her old cabin, and she just had to walk down the road toward the horse barn. She joined the other girls in blue dresses, each of them fiddling with some part of their outfit. The flowers in their hair, the straps on their shoes, or the sleeves on their dresses.

Adele didn't fidget or flinch, because she'd just caught sight of Carson.

And wow, he looked amazing in those dark slacks, white shirt, and blue tie. The same blue as in the dress she wore. He adjusted his cowboy hat just as someone said, "Get in line, guys. Scarlett and Hudson are almost here."

Everyone paired up immediately, and it was like they'd had a ranch meeting about it, because she was left out...and so was Carson.

She glanced around, panic pounding through her as he turned in a slow circle, finally realizing that she would be the one hanging on his arm as they walked down the aisle. As he came closer, her heart flapped around in her chest as if it had grown wings.

"Looks like we're together," he drawled in that sexy voice he possessed.

In that moment, Adele realized she'd made a grave mistake. She'd suspected it before, but it was easy to push aside, behind the countless orders and the ever-present exhaustion.

But she knew now that she'd made the biggest mistake of her life when she'd given up Carson Chatworth.

Chapter Twenty-Four

Carson kept waiting for Adele to say something, finally sighing when she continued to stare at him. He fell in step beside her, wishing this wedding was over already. Or maybe he didn't wish that. Maybe he wanted the nuptials to be stalled, so he'd have time to talk to Adele, make her understand how miserable he was without her.

And honestly, she didn't look all that happy either. Sure, she was as beautiful as ever. Sexy in a way that reached right into his stomach and pulled.

He offered her his arm, and still she stared at him. "I'll see if someone will switch," he muttered, and she practically threw her hand through his arm. A shockwave of desire hit him, and he had a very real feeling that he was going to say things he'd regret later.

He only had a moment to decide if he cared or not.

Nope, came to his mind, so he leaned down and grazed his lips along her hairline. "I miss you so, so much."

I miss you wasn't the same as *I love you*, but he felt like he'd said those three little words anyway. His throat had never been drier.

"Are you happy in New York City?" he asked next, almost desperate to know. He'd been praying for her happiness for months now, and he couldn't bear to think that God had ignored him once again.

Adele looked up at him, fear in her eyes.

"Are you going to say anything?" he asked next, sensing it was almost time to begin. Then they'd walk down the aisle and separate. She'd disappear from his life again, as easily as smoke lifted into the air.

Of course she wasn't. Frustration filled him, and he swallowed to try to get it to stay dormant. He didn't want to ruin things for Hudson and Scarlett.

"Forget it," he whispered, looking away.

"No," she said, whipping his attention back to her. "No, I'm not all that happy in New York City." She swallowed but kept going. "I miss you terribly."

Hope soared through Carson. "I'm in love with you, Adele," he whispered just as the wedding march started and the couples in front of him and Adele started walking.

Her hand on his arm tightened, but he couldn't suck back in the words. He also couldn't stall the wedding without ruining it or taking the attention from where it rightfully belonged. So he stepped down the gravel lane that served as a wedding aisle, the trees towering overhead as silent sentinels.

At the altar, Adele held onto him for an extra heartbeat and then moved to the left with the other bridesmaids. Carson went right, but he didn't take his eyes from her. Had she heard him? Maybe she'd tightened her hand on his arm so she wouldn't fall on the uneven ground while wearing heels.

The ceremony was lovely and when Scarlett and Hudson kissed, he cheered along with everyone else. The party moved into the barn, and Carson got jostled in the crowd. He couldn't get over to Adele before he entered the barn to soft, party music.

Lights hung in the loft, and soft, white Christmas lights filled the rafters and were wound around the poles. The floor had been swept clean, and several long tables held refreshments near the back wall.

Scarlett and Hudson started to dance, and Carson scanned the space for Adele. He had to find her, and the need was so strong, it felt like he was suffocating.

The song ended, and Hudson stepped over to a microphone in the corner. "Thank you all for being here," he said, his voice coming from the speakers hanging up high. An idea came to Carson's mind, and he didn't dwell on it.

He acted instead, moving swiftly through the crowd until he was only feet from the microphone too. Hudson said a few more things, and then he motioned for Scarlett to come forward and say something.

Carson caught her eye, and an entire conversation happened in that single breath. She nodded once, her permission for him to steal her spotlight for just a moment.

So he darted forward and gripped the microphone with both hands, as if he was strangling a snake. "Hey," he said, his voice louder than he'd anticipated. He backed up a couple of inches. "I just wanted to add my congratulations to Hudson and Scarlett." He glanced at both of them, his nerves almost out of courage.

"And I wanted to let Adele Woodruff know that I'm not all that happy in Shiloh Ridge either. I mean, it's fine, but it's nothing like what we have here. This is a great ranch." He drew in a breath to tame his quivering emotions. "And I want to come back here, but I simply can't do it without you, Adele."

The crowd parted, showing the curvy, beautiful woman in blue that he knew he couldn't live without. Tears streamed down her face, and Carson left the microphone and strode toward her.

"Don't cry," he murmured when he reached her. He took her face in his hands and wiped her tears. "Please don't cry."

"It's a wedding," she said. "People cry."

Carson felt like crying himself, but the party around him continued. Scarlett spoke into the microphone, and people started getting food from the tables in the back.

"Can you please say something?" he asked. He'd said

so much, and he wasn't sure if she was crying because he'd embarrassed her or for some other reason.

"I'm in love with you, too," she said. "And I'd love for you to be my billionaire boyfriend again." She tipped up onto her toes and pressed her lips to his. "My *last* billionaire boyfriend."

Carson kissed her, sure he was dreaming. Then his mind caught up to his emotions, and he pulled away. "Did you just propose to me?" he asked, chuckling.

"Well, if you don't want the job." Her eyes twinkled as she shrugged one shoulder.

"Oh, I want the job." He leaned down and kissed her again, feeling more complete after only a few minutes with her in his arms than he had in over eight months.

Thank you, Lord, he prayed. *Thank you so much for answering my prayers.*

CARSON RETURNED TO SHILOH RIDGE, a bounce in his step that everyone could see. It wasn't like he was trying to hide it, and he had to talk to Bear and let him know he'd be leaving the farm.

Carson was ready for sunnier skies by the time he'd finished up his last day on the dairy farm and packed up everything he owned. Again. He was so tired of packing and driving to a new ranch, and he hoped that Last Chance Ranch would be his final destination.

He'd toyed with buying a place of his own, but he'd decided he didn't want the responsibility. He just wanted to get up and go to work, especially if that work included watching Adele do yoga in a pair of stretchy pants. He just wanted the time to spend with Adele. Build a family with her. Make a life together.

He wasn't exactly sure what her schedule was that day, but she should've left New York City yesterday. She'd said she'd call him when she was back in California, but she hadn't. He'd woken to a text that said, *It was so late I didn't call. But I'm here. Going to sleep forever.*

So he hadn't called her back. While they'd danced at the wedding, she'd confessed to him that she'd never been so tired, and she couldn't wait to return to a slower pace of life.

Carson had been surprised by that, because Adele seemed to fill her time with busy things, even when she didn't have to. The cooking, the editing, the videos. She'd told him she wanted to take the control over those back, and that she'd thought having more money to make the videos "better" would be a good thing.

He'd told her that money made some things easier, but it didn't make everything better. Now, he was just trying to figure out how he could ask her to marry him, and how he was going to live on that ranch with her without being able to go home to her at night, and where they might live once they did get married.

She hadn't brought up any of those things either, and

he'd followed her lead. Number one, he'd seen how busy she was in New York City, and that was before the restaurant had even opened. He couldn't imagine what her life was like now.

"I think that's it," he said to Bear, who'd been helping him carry boxes to the truck. "Thank you so much, Bear."

"Come back anytime," the man said as they shook hands. "You're a good cowboy, Carson."

"Thanks, Bear." He smiled into the sun, got behind the wheel, and drove as fast as he dared. He wouldn't be able to make the trip to California in one day, but it would be three before he'd pull into Last Chance Ranch again, and that moment couldn't come fast enough.

Thankfully, he had Ted and Tony to keep him company, yowl along with him as he sang the lyrics to his favorite country songs, and sleep against his back in the uncomfortable hotel rooms.

He finally rumbled up the road, the sight of that quirky robot mailbox bringing an instant smile to his face. His arms had been bent so they were in front of his see-through chest cavity, and he held a sign that said, "Welcome home, Carson!" in bright red, hand-drawn letters.

"Look at that, guys," he said to the dogs, and while they wore grins on their canine faces, he didn't think it was because of the sign.

Scarlett had said he could have his old cabin back, and he turned down the first road he came to on the ranch. He knew instantly that something was afoot, because the road was lined with goats of all sizes. They'd been tied to stakes in the ground and carefully positioned.

He slowed and rolled down his windows. The scent of this place filled his nose, and it was wonderful and familiar, like freshly mowed grass and spring sunshine. Scarlett and Hudson sat in the back of his truck, and they waved him down the road.

Cache stood at the back of the truck, and he waved too. Carson turned and pulled into his driveway, already laughing when he got out of the truck and brought his backpack with him. Everyone was there to greet him, a whole party of people sitting on the front steps of his cabin. People he knew from the last time he'd been here. People he didn't.

It didn't matter. If you came to Last Chance Ranch, you became family. The sight of Adele smiling at him made Carson's heart pinch, and he crossed the lawn to her and swept her off her feet as they both laughed.

"You're something else, you know that?" he asked.

"Yeah, well, hold onto your hat, cowboy," she said as he set her on her feet. "We're just getting started."

Chapter Twenty-Five

Someone had definitely shoved loaded cannons down Adele's throat, and they were all firing. She hated how Carson made her so tongue-tied, especially since they'd started getting along. She'd had no problem yelling at him to get away from her cabin and move his truck so she could back out of her parking space at the grocery store.

"There's more?" Carson asked.

"So much more." Adele smiled through her nerves and laced her fingers through Carson's. "Now, I know you like everything to be nice and neat, but well, I may have done a little extraneous decorating for your welcome home party."

"Oh, boy," Carson said, walking slowly with her toward the steps. They went past everyone there, all of whom wore goofy grins on their faces. Adele had made

Hudson, Cache, and Scarlett stay the furthest away, because none of them had a good enough poker face. As it was, Carson knew something was going on.

"The goat line-up was impressive," he said. "Did you do that?"

"I thought of it, but Amber executed it. You should see her with the goats. It's like they speak the same language." Adele shook her head. "She's agreed to give us goat yoga back as long as she can keep visiting them."

"I don't see how that's a problem," he said. "How do you feel about learning to horseback ride?"

Adele's first reaction was to say no, but she shrugged one shoulder instead. "If you insist. Do they have ladders to help me get on the horse?" Because she knew she couldn't heave herself into a saddle. It looked easy, but Adele knew it wasn't.

They reached the door, and her pulse skipped and leaped inside her chest. She put her palm flat against the wood and said, "Okay, here we go."

She closed her eyes for a moment, drew in a deep breath, and twisted the doorknob. She stepped inside just far enough to give Carson room to follow her. The balloons she'd driven to town to get drifted in the breeze from the open windows, and the scent of sugar and chocolate and coffee filled the small space.

"Welcome home, cowboy," she said. "I made all the food, and I don't think there's anything better than balloons."

"There's not," he said, gazing around. "Tony and Ted are going to hate you though. They're terrified of balloons." He laughed, the sound full of joy and love. "This is great, Adele."

"I'm glad you like it."

Other people entered the house, and Adele felt her opportunity slipping away. They'd take the brownies and pour the coffee, and her voice would fade into the chatter a party produced.

Scarlett came inside, and she said, "You better ask him before Dave steals him away."

Adele wiped her hands down the front of her jeans and stepped over to the kitchen counter, where Carson was already engrossed in a conversation with Dave. He stood a few feet from the jewelry box she'd placed right next to the cupcake tower, and he hadn't even noticed it.

She picked up the box and said in the loudest voice she could muster, "I just have one more thing to say."

Everyone looked at her, and Adele almost bolted for the back door. Instead, she moved right in front of Carson and held out the ring box. "I love you, and I was hoping—"

"Wait, wait," he said, backing up into the counter. "What is this?" He glanced around, but Adele didn't need to. Everyone's face seemed to be engrained in her mind's eye.

Horror filled her. "This is me asking you to marry me."

"No, no." Carson laughed, and Adele prayed for the floor to open up and swallow her whole.

"No?" She cocked her hip, some of her Southern fire flaring to life. "So you lure me back—?"

"You can't ask me to marry you," he said, striding over to the couch where he'd deposited his backpack. He unzipped one pocket and then the next, Adele glancing around at the others in the cabin. Scarlett caught her eye and lifted her eyebrows as if to say, *What's he doing?*

But Adele didn't know.

"Ah, here it is." He pulled something out of the bag and faced her again. "I wasn't sure when I'd be using this, and I was hoping to have a speech prepared." He swallowed and glanced around. "But you started it." He brought his hand out from behind his back and produced a ring box. "I bought this in Texas, because I was hoping you and I, well, will you marry me?"

Adele stared at the diamond in the box, and it was definitely the cut, size, and clarity a billionaire would procure for the woman he loved. Her heart beat like a strobe in her chest, and she pressed one hand over it.

"Carson."

"That's not a yes."

"You already told me no," she said.

"No," he said. "I didn't want you to ask me." He took another step toward her, that huge diamond still between them. "I wanted to ask you."

"Well, you got what you wanted."

"Not yet." He shook the ring box.

Adele looked at it, and then him, and then leaned over

to really study the ring. Teasing him was so much fun, especially when his blue eyes darkened.

She sighed. "Oh, all right. I'll marry you."

"Yeah?" The hope and light in his face made her smile.

"Yeah." Adele laughed and threw herself into Carson's arms. She loved the spicy, warm scent of him, the way he held her so close to him, like he couldn't get her near enough.

He laughed with her, then stepped back and slid the ring on her finger, and grinned as he lifted her hand up for everyone to see. "She said yes!"

A cheer went up, and Adele's face heated as he tucked her against his side. "Now, I saw cupcakes over there that look suspiciously close to that video you posted last week, and I think there are peanut butter cups inside them. Can we have one of those now?"

THE WHOLE RANCH boasted navy blue, silver, red, and green. A single poinsettia bloom hung from every fence post, and Prime held silver bells in his outstretched hands. Garland hung between the flowers, and once again, the horse barn had more Christmas lights than probably all the trees in LA.

Because Adele and Carson were getting married today.

She currently sat in the saddle of a black and white horse, the air chilly as the sun rose into the sky. The gray gave way to orange and gold and then blue. The silence between her, the sky, and Carson was the most wonderful thing in the world, and she wanted to hold onto it forever.

But they headed back to the stables, brushed down the horses, and put them in the pasture. Carson swept his arm around her waist and leaned down to kiss the top of her head. Even through the straw hat she wore everywhere, she felt the heat from his mouth.

"I can't wait to marry you," he said.

"Only a couple more hours now." She smiled up at him. "I can't wait to get to Portugal."

"It'll be warmer than here," he said.

"No talk about the weather," she said. "No, what I want to talk about is the food. The beaches. I bought two new swimming suits."

"Oh, now I'm interested in the beach."

"I can't believe you don't like the beach."

"It's not that I don't like it. I've never been."

"Yes, we went several times over the summer." Adele loved lying on the warm sand, listening to the waves roll in. Loved snacking on grapes and sliced red peppers and potato chips while the sun sank into the ocean.

"I've never been in Portugal."

"I told you we could take an Alaskan cruise."

"In December?" He scoffed like they hadn't discussed

their honeymoon at length. Several times. "Portugal is fine."

"Fine."

"I didn't mean that. It's great." He moved in front of her. "Anywhere with you will be wonderful. Paradise. Heaven." He leaned down and kissed her until Adele felt lightheaded, and she stumbled back to her cabin to get ready to make her billionaire boyfriend into her cowboy husband.

And she was going to make sure he loved the beach by the time they left Portugal.

"READY?" Scarlett asked.

"Ready," Adele confirmed. She let her mother fix the veil one more time, and then they all left her tiny cabin. The horse-drawn carriage waited outside her back door, and the three of them got in, Adele fluffing and fixing the skirt of her dress even though it was just a short three-minute ride over to the barn.

Warm light spilled from the open doors, the scent of flowers and sugar in the air. She'd made her own wedding cake, but she'd allowed Scarlett and Jeri to cater the rest of the event.

Just inside the barn, Adele paused. Large glass containers lined one table to her right, and they held yellow, pink, and peach lemonades. They glinted under the lights, making Adele's breath catch.

"Stay here," Scarlett said, hurrying down the aisle. A sense of anxiety hit her hard. She wasn't terribly close with her father, but he came toward her with a huge smile on his face.

"Baby." He kissed her cheek.

"Hey, Daddy." She held onto his arm like it was her lifeline, because in that moment, it literally was. The aisle was short, and the music inside the barn stopped.

Everyone stood and turned toward her. Adele smiled the way she'd practiced, still somewhat in a state of shock that she was here for a second time when she'd vowed she'd never get married again.

She stepped with her father, no bridal party going in front of her. Just Carson waiting at the altar, which was a sawhorse with flowers on it. Her eyes locked onto his, and all her fears, doubts, and panic faded away. She loved him. He loved her.

Nothing else mattered.

Her father transferred her hand from his arm to Carson's, patted it, and went to take his seat.

Adele listened to Pastor Williams talk about love and forgiveness, about second chances and being a united team. Adele wanted to do all of those things, and every breath felt like it might be the one to make her burst.

But she didn't. She kissed Carson after she was proclaimed his wife, and giggles poured from her. It was her expression of happiness—of joy—and she tipped up on her toes and said, "I love you so much." She leaned her forehead against his. "Thank you for letting me have wings to go to New York. Thank you for being my safe place to fall. Thank you for coming back to Last Chance Ranch to be *my* last chance."

Carson simply looked into her eyes, a softness in his that spoke of how much he adored her. Then he simply said, "I love you, Adele. You're welcome."

Read on for a sneak peek at the next book in this series,
LAST CHANCE WEDDING.

Sneak Peek! Last Chance Wedding - Chapter 1

J eri Bell whistled as she put on her tool belt, the cheery California sunshine lighting the day beyond her bedroom window. The days she didn't get to work on a construction site were a waste of time in her opinion, and she'd had a lot of those lately.

"But not anymore," she said to herself as she started gathering her copious amounts of hair into a ponytail. She knew most women would kill to have as much hair as she did, especially as hers held a curl like it was the eighties and it hadn't gotten the memo.

Now, she worked at Last Chance Ranch, and they needed dozens of buildings built or remodeled. She was working on the new dog enclosures first, because that would allow Scarlett and the ranch more room to house more animals. And more animals was good for the partnership they had with Forever Friends, who provided a lot of grant money for the ranch.

In fact, Forever Friends provided the salary Jeri had named, right down to the penny. Of course, she'd given an even dollar amount, so there were no pennies. She grinned at herself, burying the vein of guilt that was open and never seemed to close.

She brushed it aside like she'd been doing for a few months now, since she'd come to the ranch and started surveying the land, putting in quotes, and beginning the construction.

Her crew was usually at least a dozen men, and she'd become extraordinarily good at managing them over the past twenty years of her life. But out here, it was her and whichever cowboy she could scrounge from his regular chores if there was something that required more than two hands.

That was almost always Hudson, Scarlett's boyfriend, or Sawyer, the cowboy who lived right next door to her. Jeri looked south as if she had superpowers and could see through cabin walls to the cowboy's place next door.

He had an amazing dog that followed him around the ranch like, well, a puppy, and Jeri mourned the loss of her canine. The chickens she'd brought with her hardly counted as pets, as one of them had a crazy eye that seemed to look everywhere but where it was going. Still, she loved Spot and Feathers, and she left her ponytail to be bumpy so she could go feed them before she hurried over to the construction site.

Her yard wasn't fenced, but the chickens never seemed to stray too far from the source of their food, and Jeri found them at the bottom of the steps just outside the back door, clucking away.

"Hey, guys," she said, reaching for the wooden lid on the box she'd built to keep the feed in. She grabbed a handful and scattered it over the grass near them. Spot did his funky chicken run as he went after the food.

She laughed at them and threw more feed than they needed. Feathers, a brown and black chicken, would try to follow her over to the construction site. Then she'd realize that it was way too far for her two short feet, and she'd eventually make her way back to the yard.

"I'm going to get that house finished," she promised them, looking at the half-finished coop Scarlett had given her permission to build. "I am. Tonight. I'll work on it tonight."

She was usually exhausted by the time she finished over in Canine Club, and really, she was never finished. She worked until her back ached and she reached a spot where she could pick up the next day. But by the time she got home, she was lucky to stick something in the microwave and collapse on the couch after eating it.

So her diet wasn't the best. She often skipped breakfast and lunch, drinking only water so she didn't faint in the summer heat as she hammered and measured and nailed.

While she worked a lot, she hadn't lost much weight, because her eating habits crammed all her calories—high-density ones—into one meal.

It was fine. It was her life again, and she was grateful for that. In fact, she thought, *Thank you for bringing me here* as she walked away from the chickens and around to the dirt road in front of her cabin. She couldn't help glancing at Sawyer's front door, where sometimes the cowboy sat on the steps with his Australian shepherd at his feet and his guitar balanced against the post holding up the porch.

Whenever he sat outside at night and played, Jeri would make sure her windows were open. A few times she'd even gone out onto her back porch and listened to him sing in his beautiful tenor voice.

So maybe she had a little crush on the cowboy next door. Maybe.

Her heart pumped out an extra beat, and she reminded herself that she had done the boyfriend thing. The husband thing. The family thing. The in-a-new-relationship-with-someone-she-worked-with thing.

And she wasn't going to do any of it again.

The price was too high—and she knew. She'd lost everything over the years, and she could only count on herself to rebuild her life.

Which is what I'm doing, she thought as she caught

sight of Hudson's truck rounding the corner and coming toward her. She put a smile on her face and waved to him as he passed, because through her divorce, the loss of her business, her crew, and all of her friends, she'd learned that it was easier to smile than to frown.

Scarlett had often said how much she appreciated how bubbly and optimistic Jeri was around the ranch, and Jeri appreciated the comments. She wasn't exactly faking, but she did like looking at the bright side of things more than the dark. The glass was half-full and not half-empty.

After all, she'd picked herself up from some pretty awful things. Things she didn't want to think about right now.

No, right now, she needed to get the inside walls of the third dog enclosure up. When the structures were finished, they'd be temperature regulated, but right now they weren't. She worked through the morning, sweating and replacing the fluids with as much water as her stomach and bladder could hold.

She knew it was lunch only because the sun shone directly overhead—and Scarlett brought her a chicken Caesar salad.

Something was up. The owner was nice, and Jeri considered Scarlett a friend. Probably the best female friend Jeri had ever had. But she didn't bring Jeri food very often, so Jeri asked, "What's going on?" as she took the salad and the plastic fork from her boss.

Scarlett sighed and looked around the enclosure.

"Wow, it's hot in here."

"Yeah," Jeri said, opening the salad and pouring the dressing over it. "Thanks for getting this. Why'd you go down to town?"

"I was meeting with Jewel."

Jeri stuffed her mouth full of lettuce and parmesan so she could buy herself some time to answer.

"She wants to make sure all of our paperwork is up to date," Scarlett said.

"And you need my license," Jeri said, licking her fork like there wasn't a problem. She could produce her non-existent contractor's license in a jiffy. No big deal.

Except it was a big deal. Her application had been turned down again, and the salad suddenly tasted sour. An image of her former foreman filled her mind—Brenden Evans. If she could just get a hearing with the committee, she could give her side of the story.

But she already had, and they'd still taken her license away.

The only way she could get a new license was to use a different name. But she needed legal documentation with the name, and the only way to get that was to lie, or pay for forged documents, or get married.

She couldn't do the first two, because she didn't need to go to jail on top of everything else. She still went to church every chance she got, and she'd begged the Lord for a solution that was legal and would allow her to keep building this life at Last Chance Ranch.

If she could find someone willing to marry her just for a few months....

Just like all the other times she'd thought about this exact thing, no one came to mind. Most sane men didn't just marry female carpenters for a favor.

"I'll go check on the status of it tomorrow," Jeri said, forking another bite of chicken and lettuce into her mouth. She chewed and swallowed. "Maybe I did something wrong."

"We just need the application and where it is," Scarlett said, still looking around. "This is going so great, Jeri."

She put that smile on her face, nodded, and said, "Thanks." She stirred her salad around, the ever-present guilt blooming and growing into a raging river in her system.

She knew the status of her contractor license, and all she could do was apply again. Make up a little white lie about how she'd done something wrong and had to re-file, and give Scarlett that application status.

It would buy her another few weeks, at least.

Scarlett said goodbye and left the half-finished enclosure, leaving Jeri to her worries and doubts. She couldn't eat any more salad—number one, she disliked salad. Number two, she wasn't used to eating in the middle of the day.

She got back to work. Decided to stop while it was still light—and before she lopped off a thumb because she couldn't focus. Her mind hadn't stopped circling her problem, and she still had no idea what to do about it.

Her stomach growled as she walked back to the main road and around to the Cabin Community. Her feet crunched against the gravel, and she went through every able-bodied man she knew. Before the disaster that had lost her the license, she would've had a crew of fifteen men she could ask for a favor like this.

Now, while she liked this life a lot, she didn't have anyone the way she used to. No one to really call on in a sticky situation like the one she currently found herself in.

Loneliness engulfed her, and she turned down the driveway that led to her back yard when she heard the clucking.

Up the steps her feet took her, and she went in the front door, her thoughts turning to dinner and what she had in the freezer. Three steps inside the cabin, she realized something was very wrong.

This didn't smell like her house.

"Hullo, Jeri," a man said, causing her to yelp and spin toward the sound. Her heart banged against her ribs as she realized she wasn't staring at an enemy, but Sawyer Smith.

She'd gone in the wrong house. She scanned him from head to toe, noticing his hair was damp and curling in a very sexy way around his ears. He looked totally different without that cowboy hat on his head, and every female part in Jeri started rejoicing that she'd made this particular mistake.

Sneak Peek! Last Chance
Wedding - Chapter 2

"Sawyer," Jeri said, scanning him again, and Sawyer felt like he'd put his shirt on backward. Checked and everything. His clothes looked right, zipper was zipped up, all of that.

"I was just thinking," she said, her voice like music to his ears. "I guess I came in the wrong house." Her wide eyes softened, and she laughed, driving Sawyer's thoughts into a frenzy.

He's been texting with his mother about the family picnic at his childhood home in Newport Beach, and she'd been pressing him about who he was bringing. As if showing up to a family event alone wouldn't be tolerated.

Of course, for his family, it wasn't. He'd taken so many women to events, it was a miracle he hadn't simply kept one of them as a girlfriend.

"It's fine," he said, chuckling with her. "I did just shower, but I'm dressed, obviously." Why was he talking about showering? His face heated, and he didn't say he'd only gotten in the shower so he wouldn't be able to text.

He'd prayed for a solution to his problem, and the next thing he knew, Jeri had walked in his house. Was she the answer to his family situation? Would she be willing to drive a couple of hours south for some bad potato salad and an overcooked hamburger?

Why couldn't he ask her?

He'd asked probably half a dozen other women to stand in as his girlfriend in the past.

Probably because you'd like to take her out for real, he thought.

"Obviously," she said, her eyes still crinkled with laughter. He sure did like her jovial attitude and hard-working spirit. He'd lived next door to her for just over three weeks, and he'd already asked out another woman here and been turned down.

Sort of. Adele was dating Carson, but Sawyer hadn't realized that when he'd asked her to dinner. Was Jeri dating someone he didn't know about?

He didn't know, and he wasn't going to ask. He hadn't dated anyone seriously for a long time, but he knew there were some rules to dating and asking point blank if someone had a girlfriend wasn't how it was done.

"You want to stay for dinner?" he asked. "I put one of those frozen enchilada meals in when I got home."

"Oh, I don't need to do that," she said, turning back to the door. "I'm sure I have pizza or something in my freezer."

"So you could eat my freezer food just as easily as yours," he said, wondering if that was obvious enough for her. Heat spiraled through his body, his air conditioning struggling to keep up with the hot California summer as it was.

No matter what, he didn't want her to leave quite yet. He wanted to go to the picnic, if only to get off the ranch for a couple of days. He loved Last Chance Ranch, he did. But he'd been here for seven years, and sometimes he missed the beach, a society where there were more people than animals, and a faster pace of life.

He'd left horse racing for a reason, and he reminded himself of it each time he started to feel antsy on the ranch. His parents lived only a couple of hours away, and it was the perfect distance for a weekend trip to remind himself of how much he loved the quiet peace of the foothills where the ranch was located.

"I guess," Jeri said, something sparking between them. He wasn't sure what it was. He'd waved to Jeri loads of times. Spoken to her and admired her beauty from thirty yards away, standing on his porch while she stood on hers.

She'd never given him any indication that she was interested in him—or anyone really. Sawyer had lived on the earth long enough to know that everyone had a story, a past, especially when they got to be as old as him and Jeri.

Not that he even know how old she was. He wanted to find out, and his fingers tingled in anticipation as he moved into the kitchen to check on his pre-made dinner. They could spend hours together in the truck, getting to know one another, as they drove down to Newport Beach.

"Looks like it's almost done," he said, though he had no idea. The timer said ten minutes, so he figured it *was* almost done. "How are the chickens?"

"Just fine," she said, glancing around. "Where's Blue?"

"Oh, he's outside somewhere," Sawyer said, unconcerned. "Hudson was saddling up, and he thought maybe he'd go with him." Sawyer grinned at her, suddenly self-conscious about the state of his cabin. He wasn't the neatest man on the planet, and now every item that sat out of place bothered him.

He opened a drawer and swept the dental floss and tape sitting on the counter into it, trying to find something else to ask her about. "So, Jeri, what did you do before you came to the ranch?"

"I owned a construction company," she said, and Sawyer turned around to find her stepping into the kitchen. The cabin was nice, and he was happy for the housing, but it wasn't exactly high-end. He gestured to the dining room table that only had two chairs, and she moved over to it and sat.

"Your own company," he said. "That's great. You don't anymore?"

"No," she said, shaking her head, an edge entering her eyes. "Not anymore."

"I sense a story there."

"Oh, there's a story." She flashed him a smile that only lit her face halfway. How he knew that, he wasn't sure. Oh, yes, he was. He'd been watching her for a while now. "But I don't want to tell it tonight."

"Fair enough," he said. "Maybe you'll tell me another time."

"Sure," she said, but he detected a bit of falseness in her voice.

His phone buzzed, and they both looked at it. "It's my mother," he said, sighing. "She's having a big barbecue this weekend, and she'd bugging me about coming."

"You don't want to go?" Jeri asked.

"I do," Sawyer said slowly, trying to get the words to line up right inside his mouth. "My family is a bit...peculiar."

"All families are," she said. "My nearest sibling is ten years older than me. I'm the caboose baby."

"Wow," he said. "And how old is that?"

Their eyes caught again, and he smiled at her this time as the electricity pulsed between them.

"My older brother, Ricky, is fifty-two."

So she was even older than him, and Sawyer wasn't sure why, but he did like that. "I'm the middle child," he said. "One older sister. One younger brother. Rosie's married with a couple of kids."

The timer on the oven interrupted them, and Sawyer seized the opportunity to walk away from Jeri, trying to center his thoughts. It certainly was easier when she wasn't so close, perfuming the air with sawdust and something floral.

"Anyway," he said. "My mother is...neurotic about significant others." He pulled the pan of enchiladas out of the oven, almost dropping the tented foil lid on the floor in the process.

"Meaning?" Jeri asked, joining him in the kitchen. She opened two cupboards before she found the plates, and she pulled down two.

"Meaning we don't go to family events without a guest. A partner. A...girlfriend." He swallowed, and he couldn't seem to look away from her. She pulled a couple of forks out of the drawer next to the fridge and faced him.

"Are you asking me to be your guest?" Her eyes danced with amusement. "Partner? Girlfriend?" She pealed out another wave of laughter, and Sawyer joined her.

"No, of course not."

"Oh, who'd you ask?"

"I, uh, haven't asked anyone. I probably won't go." His phone buzzed again, and Jeri glanced back to the table where he'd left it.

"That's too bad," Jeri said, retreating out of the kitchen, giving him room to breathe and work. "I kinda like family picnics."

"Do you?" He stared at her. Maybe he'd messed up already. "It's this weekend," he said. "Like, in two days. It's a couple hours of driving. Each way." He wasn't sure why he was trying to talk her out of it instead of into it.

"Well, if you can't get anyone else to go, I'm free." She shrugged those sexy shoulders, the purple straps of her tank top covering her bronzed skin in thin strips.

"Let's plan on it then," he said, his throat raw. He kept his eyes down as he served them each a couple of enchiladas. He slid a plate in front of her and sat down in his spot. "We don't have to leave too terribly early. Maybe like nine or ten."

Jeri smiled at him, and Sawyer couldn't believe things had worked out so easily. He hadn't had to make a fool of himself on her front steps, and he could pretend like he didn't have budding feelings for her, the way he'd been doing.

Still, when their eyes met again, that charge roared to life for the third time. Without hesitating, he said, "Maybe we can go to dinner tomorrow night," he said. "Get to know each other better before we have to hold hands in front of my family."

Jeri dropped her fork with a clatter, her eyes widening again. "Hold hands?"

He chuckled, which relieved some of the tension. "Well, it's been a while since I've had a girlfriend, I'll admit. But I'm pretty sure the kids are holding hands still."

She picked up her fork and cut a bite of enchilada. "I

mean, I heard you say girlfriend. I guess I just wasn't expecting...." She let her voice trail into silence, and now she wore a calculating look.

"It would just be for an afternoon," he said, his spirits falling. She didn't like him. The heat between them was just him. One-sided.

A dog barked outside, and he got up to let Blue in. "There you are, bud," he said. "C'mon in."

"Hey, Blue." Jeri let the Australian shepherd come over to her and she scrubbed him down in hello. "Can he eat enchiladas?"

"I'm sure he can," Sawyer said, liking the way she interacted with his dog. He wasn't sure why everything Jeri did seemed dipped in gold, but her feeding Blue a bit of chicken and cheese seriously got Sawyer's heart thumping in his chest.

The conversation moved to happenings around the ranch, and Jeri stayed for another hour before saying, "I've bothered you all night," and getting to her feet.

"It wasn't a bother," Sawyer said, walking her to the front door. He opened it for her and stepped back, grinning at her in what he hoped was a friendly, next-door-neighborly way.

"So dinner tomorrow." She looked up at him, hope shining in her eyes. And she hadn't asked. "I love that bistro on Clover Street. Have you been there?"

"No, ma'am."

She swatted at his bicep, a laugh following. "I may be old, Mister, but I'm not a ma'am."

"You're not old," he said, hoping he still knew how to flirt.

"Older than you, I'm sure."

"A few years," he said, shrugging. "I'm thirty-eight."

She nodded, her smile revealing her pretty white teeth. "What time tomorrow? I tend to get lost on a project and I don't remember to look at a clock."

"Seven?" It had been a *really* long time since he'd been out with someone. Longer than he wanted to admit.

"Sure, seven." She shuffled forward and stepped back. "All right. See you then." She committed to leaving then, and stepped fully out onto the porch.

"Bye," he said as she went down the steps and across the lawn to her house. He sighed and picked up his guitar from its spot just inside the door. For the first time in a very long time, he didn't feel like the evening hours were too long.

His fingers plucked a tune out of the strings without him thinking about it, and he hummed a love song in the back of his throat, his thoughts centered firmly on the beautiful Jeri Bell.

Can she risk her heart—and her business—again? Find out in **Last Chance Wedding!**

Scan the QR code for a direct link to the paperback.

Last Chance Ranch Romance series

Journey to Last Chance Ranch and meet curvy, mature women looking for love later in life. Experience sisterhood, goat yoga, and a fake marriage against a stunning, inspirational ranch background—and some sexy cowboys too— from USA Today bestseller and Top 10 Kindle All-Star author Liz Isaacson!

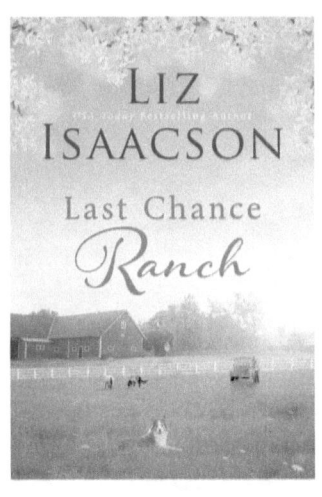

Last Chance Ranch (Book 1): A cowgirl down on her luck hires a man who's good with horses and under the hood of a car. Can Hudson fine tune Scarlett's heart as they work together? Or will things backfire and make everything worse at Last Chance Ranch?

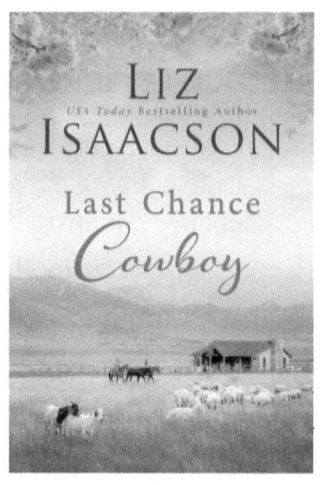

Last Chance Cowboy (Book 2): A billionaire cowboy without a home meets a woman who secretly makes food videos to pay her debts...Can Carson and Adele do more than fight in the kitchens at Last Chance Ranch?

Last Chance Wedding (Book 3): A female carpenter needs a husband just for a few days... Can Jeri and Sawyer navigate the minefield of a pretend marriage before their feelings become real?

Last Chance Reunion (Book 4): An Army cowboy, the woman he dated years ago, and their last chance at Last Chance Ranch... Can Dave and Sissy put aside hurt feelings and make their second chance romance work?

Last Chance Lake (Book 5): A former dairy farmer and the marketing director on the ranch have to work together to make the cow cuddling program a success. But can Karla let Cache into her life? Or will she keep all her secrets from him - and keep *him* a secret too?

Last Chance Christmas (Book 6): She's tired of having her heart broken by cowboys. He waited too long to ask her out. Can Lance fix things quickly, or will Amber leave Last Chance Ranch before he can tell her how he feels?

About Liz

Liz Isaacson writes inspirational romance, usually set in Texas, or Montana, or anywhere else horses and cowboys exist. She lives in Utah, where she walks her dogs daily, watches a lot of Netflix, and eats a lot of peanut butter M&Ms while writing. Find her on her website at feelgood-fictionbooks.com.